From the Kiwi Kingdom Series

# THE  DRIFTWOOD SHORE

By

Rosemary Thomas

*For Juneybee.*

*Love*

*Rosemary x4*

OTHER BOOKS BY ROSEMARY THOMAS in the Kiwi Kingdom Series:

- Under the Blowholes Spray
- The Islands
- Beneath The Long White Cloud

The Kiwi Kingdom is also on Facebook.

Information about the publishing of titles by the Author can be found on this page. Organisations that care for Kiwi and other animals in the real Kiwi Kingdom are also promoted on this page.

ISBN: 9780648740629   Paperback edition

ABN: 61517596692

The Driftwood Shore by Rosemary Thomas

Front Cover photograph by the Author

Printed and bound in Australia by Ingram Spark. First Printing, August 2020

Contact for Author: rosemarythomas19@hotmail.com

Information used for the story in this title is from the following sources:

Maori Wedding traditions in New Zealand – Wedding guide.co.nz.

Reeds Lilliput Dictionary, Maori – English, English – Maori.

# THE DRIFTWOOD SHORE

# THE YEARS BETWEEN

"Look out! We are coming through!" Michael called as he and Lucy negotiated the steep slope on the biking trail. With a smile Amy and Brett pulled over to let their children pass.

"It doesn't seem that long since they were running around on their tricycles." Brett commented.

"Yes," Amy agreed. "and it won't be long before they get their licences and be heading off for their studies."

"We can look forward to having the house to ourselves again!" Brett looked at Amy with his special smile. The passion within their relationship smouldered, not far from the surface.

"We can!" Amy agreed, answering his smile with her own. "We should try to catch up, or they will think we've got lost."

Amy didn't usually think about the past, but she was grateful now, that life had turned out as it had. Looking back at her first marriage with Terry, they had started out with similar ideals, but once he started on his career at the bank, it came before everything, including their relationship.

Amy was glad the advert for the sale of her Great Grandmother Emily's house came along to make them face the fact that they wanted to travel different paths in life. Otherwise she would never have moved to the West Coast and met Brett.

One very wet weekend, Amy had visited Lake Kaniere with her neighbour Claire, hoping to find a lost family heirloom that Emily had Left behind so long ago.

During Amy's weekend at the lake, she not only located her family heirloom, she also met the life partner she had been waiting for. His love for the outdoors was surpassed by his passion for her.

When they married, there was no question of where they were going to live. Brett was happy they already had a home to share together and didn't have to borrow a large mortgage as his mates had to do. He had some savings, intended for a home deposit; so Amy's home was renovated to make the interior the modern but comfortable family home they needed.

Their son Michael and daughter Lucy came along quickly. Amy had intended to be a full time mum at home, but the hospital was so accommodating with days and shifts, Amy was able to carry on with her career part time untill the children were at school.

Most weekends were spent out at the family bach, where Brett's parents Frank and Myrtle joined them. Given that her own parents had both passed away, Amy appreciated being accepted by Brett's family and treated like a daughter.

As the children grew into teenagers, with their father's love of the outdoors and Lucy was showing signs of talent as an artist, They had no idea of the change coming to their future.

Terry sat in his office at the bank looking out the window at the rolling adverts on the opposite building. The adverts were of driftwood sculptures at the Hokitika Beach festival.

Right now, he was feeling that both his job and his life were like the driftwood on the beach – washed up!

On the computer screen in front of him was an email from Doug his superior. Terry already knew the contents before he opened it.  After days of rumours and conjecture, his notice was formally here.  Although it was presented in positive terms – new opportunities were available for personnel who were available to relocate to their Asian outlets; however applicants with families would be given preference. Coming changes to technology also required a number of redundancies. Terry was pleased to see the redundancy offer was generous.  The fact that he had received the letter, told Terry that he was being lined up for a redundancy.  One thing Terry was glad of, he had a month to make a decision as to what he was going to do with his life.

Although Terry was feeling lonely - he didn't have a partner to talk to, about his current predicament; Terry was also glad he didn't have a wife and family to consider.

Quietly, he started to clear out his desk. Not that there was much in the way of personal items for Terry to remove. He liked the minimalist approach, which he also tried to live by at home in his unit, which was all clean lines, apart from his books which he cherished. When Terry had finished, only the essentials remained for the next person to clear up.  The remainder of the afternoon was spent going through his workload, making decisions that would normally have been left for coming weeks.

"What's up?" Doug asked at one point, after seeing  the extra activity coming from Terry's office.

Terry smiled. "I know my job's going, so I'm just making sure there aren't too many loose ends for someone else to clean up."

"Thanks." Doug looked gloomy as he spoke. "I should be doing it too."

"Your job is going too?" Terry was shocked, as he knew that Doug had a big mortgage and a family to provide for.

"It is." Doug's voice was full of despair. "I can't see the wife and my teenage children relocating to Asia. It is no use my seeking work in this sector. All the banks will be doing the same eventually. The thought of having to move house and retrain for something completely different is completely daunting at the minute. I'm not sure how I'm going to tell her and them."

"How about taking her out to dinner? It may the last one you have till you're settled into your new life."

"That's an idea! Thanks Terry."

Doug left Terry's office to phone his wife.

When Terry let himself into his apartment that evening, he took a good look around, for he knew that it would have to be sold at some point. Even though Terry owned it outright, the fees and lifestyle here couldn't be maintained without a substantial salary coming in. Terry didn't usually like to drink alone, but he made an exception this evening and took it out onto his balcony to enjoy the unobstructed vista of the harbour lights and bustle of the surrounding streets while he could. Terry thought back to when he first came to Auckland, renting a small flat in a big and noisy block, with a lift that only worked for half of the time.

After seeing a sign on a building near his work which was to be developed for luxury units, Terry made enquiries. One of the penthouse apartments was available and he could afford it. Terry revelled in having his own space that was completely to his taste.

4

The ladies that came and went from his life weren't as impressed with the "bachelor pad" Terry had created, which was too stark for their liking. The ladies also weren't impressed, that Terry's job came first in his life. They couldn't see him being the supportive husband and father to them and their family that they wanted.

When Terry checked similar properties to his on the internet, he was surprised at how much his unit had appreciated in value. He gave the local real estate agent a call, advising them that his unit would be coming on the market during the next month. The Agent arranged to inspect the unit the next day.

Terry only had to consider what he was going to do when his time at the bank ended. Then he remembered his ambition years ago to find a cottage to write the book he had planned, but never did. Terry opened a word document on his laptop and started writing.

# THE FISHING TRIP

One Friday afternoon, Amy and Lucy waved goodbye to Brett and Michael as they set out on their fishing trip for the weekend. They intended to camp at Gillespies' beach. It was only a short drive to the Fox township Hotel if the weather turned bad. Lucy would have gone with them, but Amy had promised her a shopping trip up to Greymouth. They intended to find the shoes she wanted to wear with the dress she had brought for the next Friday night dance.

The trip down to Fox Glacier took Brett and Michael through familiar forests and lakes that were now calm, waiting for the approaching evening to spread her cloak of darkness over them. In the fading light of the sunset, they set up camp at the Beach and cast their lines into the surf. A small shark was quickly hauled in and became their supper. Cooked over the camp fire, along with the tin of baked beans they had brought with them.

For Amy, Saturday morning had dawned cool and clear, with an idyllic view of the Alps to the East.. Amy knew Brett and Michael could see them too, even though their view was different to hers. Down at Gillespies Beach Brett and Michael were awake early too. The sleeping bags on the Lilo mattresses hadn't been quite as comfortable as they had hoped, so they decided to take a look at Lake Matheson before the breeze and cloud came to spoil the reflection of Mount Cook and Tasman. They spent a couple of happy hours walking the perimeter track before returning to their camp to cook up some bacon and eggs on the griddle over the camp fire.

When Brett and Michael cast their lines into the water, a fresh sea breeze had sprung up to make any catch a challenge. By dinner time there had been several nibbles but no catches. They stowed their lines away and took a trip up to the hotel for a roast dinner and a few drinks with the locals in the bar, while Michael played pool with some new friends he had met. When they finally retreated to their sleeping bags that night, the long day in the fresh air caught up with them and were soon nodding off to sleep to the sound of the waves on the nearby shore.

The next morning, the fresh breeze had strengthened enough for Brett to leave the camp fire unlit. Clouds hid the alps from view while they packed up the tent and sleeping bags. They sat in the car to watch the surf as they ate the bread and tinned corn beef sandwiches that was remaining in their food supplies.

Before they started the trip home, they took a detour up the valley to the glacier. After the steep walk up to the viewing area, both Brett and Michael wondered whether it was worth the effort; but while they were getting their breath back, the sun shone through the cloud, making the glacier dazzle.

Back at the car, Brett offered to let Michael drive. Michael had sufficient lessons for him to be confident that Michael could handle the roads on a quiet Sunday morning. Michael was due to sit his test the following week. They put his L's in position and set off. Michael was enjoying the challenge of negotiating the twists and turns of Mount Hercules. He noticed a car was approaching from the other direction, so made sure he wasn't too close to the mid line. What neither Brett nor Michael was expecting, as they came round a blind bend, was two sheep, now in the middle of their lane.

The sheep were escapees from their paddock in the valley below. The other car Michael had seen was now slowing to stop in the other lane. Michael swerved to their side of the road to avoid the sheep, only to find the car sliding off the cliff. Brett tried to reach the steering wheel to bring it back, but it was too late. The car plunged into the forested slopes below. The horrified gasp from Michael was the last sound he made in the chaos as the car and its contents tumbled and crushed in on them.

At their home, on Kaniere Road, Amy was beginning to prepare the vegetables for their meal. She expected that Brett and Michael would be back for their dinner.

"Do you want me to call them to see how long they will be?" Lucy asked, when she saw her mother making preparations.

"That's a good idea." Amy smiled.

Lucy called Michael's phone, but after ringing, was diverted to his message bank. She then rang Brett's phone. After several long rings, it was answered by a voice that she knew immediately was not her father.

"It's the police here. Who is calling?"

The gasp Lucy made and the shocked look on her face, made Amy race over to take the phone from her.

Dinner was left unmade that night. Neither Amy nor Lucy felt like eating, after receiving the news that Brett and Michael weren't ever coming back to them. Instead they curled up on the couch together as they grieved.

When their neighbour Claire heard of the accident on the evening news, she immediately came over to their house, which was in darkness. She could see Amy and Lucy huddled together on the couch.

After a quick knock to announce she was here, Claire came straight in to give them a cuddle. She was a godsend in the following days of preparing for the funeral and settling Brett's affairs. While Amy seemed to be carrying on normally, she knew she was on auto-pilot. The hospital had offered Amy some time off, but she declined for now.

"I need to keep busy, while I get through this, but I will take some later."

Lucy too was unsettled. Although she was thankful that the shopping trip had stopped her from going on the fishing trip, she was feeling guilty that she was still alive while both her father and brother were now gone. Although she found the shoes to match the dress, Lucy never went to the dance. It was many months later before the dress was worn.

Lucy was studying to follow her mother into Nursing, but was feeling completely distracted. One of the other students, Hoani was keen on her, but had to keep his feelings to himself for now. He too was mourning the loss of Michael, who had been a close friend of his. He could see her mind wasn't on the subject they were swotting for.

"I'm sorry you're having such a hard time." Hoani began. "I know it's hard to concentrate on your study now your family has gone, but if you can't do it for you, then do it for them."

Lucy didn't react to Hoani's words immediately, but when he next saw her, she displayed a grim determination that showed her concentration was back.

In Auckland, Terry was watching the news, though he too was distracted as he faced an uncertain future.

He had heard through friends that had kept in touch with Amy, that she had remarried someone called Brett and they had children, Michael and Lucy. When he heard on the news that a father and son on the West Coast had been killed in an accident, he didn't take much notice. It was only later in the evening that a friend called to ask if he had heard the news that Amy's husband and son had been killed, that he knew he had to act; that Amy needed him.

Terry immediately wrote a letter of resignation, and rang Doug his superior to advise him he wouldn't be back at the office.

"Guess what?" Doug replied. "I'm resigning too! We have found ourselves a position managing a motor camp in the Coromandel." Terry could hear the happiness in Doug's Voice and was relieved for him.

"That's great news! I hope it all goes well for you!"

"It will do. We didn't think we would get to the Coromandel till we retired."

Terry packed a couple of bags and his laptop before contacting his real estate agent to list his unit. He left a key with his neighbour and asked them to collect any mail. During the drive down to Wellington to catch the ferry to Picton, and then down through the Murchison to the West Coast, Terry had plenty of time to remember both the good and bad times he had during his relationship with Amy and wondered how she would receive him when she saw him again.

He decided, that if she sent him away, he would find a place that was nice and quiet, to continue writing the book which had been his ambition from so long ago. He didn't have to worry about income as his salary at the bank had been generous and had built up a tidy sum.

Terry would also be getting a generous severance payment now he was leaving his position. The sale of the unit would also give him a good balance to set himself up in both a home and a business.

Amy was grateful when the police came to deliver Brett's and Michael's phones to her – by some miracle they had remained intact. Amy now had some photos from their trip to keep. They were loaded to a memory stick and taken to the photo lab to be printed out and mounted in a frame.

When the day of the funeral came, it was two weeks later, after the coroner had released his findings of misadventure.  Under an overcast sky, (Amy was grateful that it didn't rain), she arrived at the church. The vicar was waiting at the door to meet her.  With him was a figure Amy recognised instantly.  Terry was here! The look of sympathy in his eyes nearly undid her.  With a deep breath Amy squared her shoulders and taking Lucy's arm in hers walked to wards them.

"Hello Reverend, Hello Terry and thank you for coming.  This is my daughter Lucy."

"Hello Lucy."  Terry said simply before moving to Amy's other side to take her other arm.

Lucy registered that the man who had walked out on her mother was here.  She had seen a photo of their wedding that her mother had tucked away in her old trunk, along with the Journals  from Alice's life.  Lucy saw Terry's look of sympathy as he looked at both her mother and her.  She didn't know whether to be angry that he had turned up without notice at a time when her mother was extra vulnerable, or to be glad that he was here to give her mother support.

Lucy decided to take the cue from her mother and accept his presence. She was grateful when Hoani and his sister Reka came and slipped into the pew next to her. During the service, Lucy couldn't help thinking of whether Terry's arrival would affect her relationship with her mother and the life they had. If he stayed around, would she be expected to accept him as a father? Depending on her exam results, Lucy would be heading to Christchurch to do her nursing training, but still hoped to come home on the weekends when shifts allowed. She realised that her mother would soon be on her own for long periods, so perhaps it was a good thing that Terry was here for her.

Brett's family were startled and wondered who was the man who had come in on Amy's arm. Only Brett's mother, Myrtle remembered that Amy had been married before, and realised that the ex-husband was here!

"Didn't waste any time!" She muttered to her husband Frank.

"You're talking about Amy?" Frank was startled at her hostility.

"No! The ex-husband! He had better treat her better this time!"

After the ceremony at the cemetery, everyone came back to Amy's house, including Terry. As they came down the drive, Terry had a feeling of being here before. Then he remembered the painting that Amy had in their house in Wellington. Orchard trees lined the drive, the old house with wrap around verandah, was well kept and surrounded by a recently mown lawn and tall fir trees to protect it. A well-stocked vegetable garden lay between the house and the barn across the yard.

Some sheep were in the two paddocks across from the barn. After taking in the scene, Terry could see why Amy wanted to live here and was wishing that his ambition hadn't got in the way of him being here too. While Lucy and Hoani were talking to Terry in the lounge, Myrtle Frank and Claire were in the kitchen helping Amy to set out the food and drinks that Amy and Claire had organised beforehand.

"You're doing well." Myrtle commented to Amy, seeing that she was holding back her emotions. Amy gave her a little smile, though her eyes were bleak.

"There is plenty of time for tears later."

"If you need a hand with the lawn or garden, just call." Frank offered.

"Thank you so much." Amy came to give Frank and Myrtle a hug.

"You are still coming for our usual dinner on Friday night?"

"What about...." Frank paused looking towards the lounge.

"I don't know what his plans are yet, but regardless," Amy's tone hardened a little. "We have already lost Brett and Michael. I am not losing you as well! You are still family and you always will be."

When it came time for everyone to leave, Terry accepted a lift with Myrtle and Frank back to Hokitika. Amy had arranged to meet up with him for lunch, for she too was free for several weeks. Amy was now on the leave she promised herself. Terry realised that Amy now displayed a reserve that wasn't in their former relationship and that he had to court her all over again.

Once back in his hotel room, Terry looked on line for real estate rentals. He couldn't take it for granted that Amy would accept him back into her life and home.

He liked what he had seen of this town and intended to stay. He just had to work out an income for himself, though there was no rush for that.

Lucy was relieved to see Terry leave with her grandparents. She had enjoyed her talk with him and heard about his life, but she wasn't yet ready to see him become part of their household.

# TERRY AND AMY'S NEW BEGINNING

Amy sat by the window of the restaurant, overlooking the Hokitika Beach and the Tasman Sea. She had mixed feelings as she waited for Terry to arrive for their lunch. She had been grateful for Terry's presence yesterday as the family said goodbye to Brett and Michael, but Amy wasn't quite sure yet whether she was ready for Terry to come back into her life.

She would never forget the way Terry chose to walk out of her life last time, so she would have to be very sure of her feelings before she allowed him back into her heart again. She noticed that he was late, something he had hated in others during the time they were together. Amy was glad she had ordered a drink and was perusing the menu while she waited.

Amy was beginning to wonder whether he had changed his mind about having lunch, when the sound of quick footsteps approaching alerted her to his arrival. For some strange reason, Amy was feeling nervous. She tried to look relaxed and gave a smile as Terry came to the table, looking anxious.

"Thank you for waiting." Terry began as he sat down. "I wouldn't have been surprised if you had left. I still hate being late or being kept waiting." Terry added sheepishly. "I've been looking at properties to rent with the agent and have just finished the paperwork."

Amy raised her eyebrows at this news. "You are here to stay?" He nodded as the waitress came to take their orders for their lunch.

"What about your job at the bank?" Amy was astonished that he was leaving it, as he had put it before everything in his life.

"Yes." Terry acknowledged Amy's thoughts. "I put the job before everything, including us, but management have decided there are too many of us in head office. I had the choice of either a post in Asia, where they wanted staff with family or take a redundancy. I chose a redundancy. It gives me plenty of time to choose what I will do with my life."

"You aren't in a relationship? And what about your life in Auckland?"

"I have a unit, which I am selling." Terry then paused; his voice was full of regret when he spoke. " I have had lady friends during my time up there, but none of them were prepared for the life that my job demanded."

Amy nodded, remembering how she had rejected the prospect of being a working mother, with their children being put in care and Terry expecting to put his job first before Amy and any family they would have.

"When I heard that you had lost both Brett and Michael, I knew you would need support. There wasn't anything to keep me up there any longer, so I came." Terry paused as their lunch arrived and they tucked into their meal. "I've only been here for a week or so, but I already feel at home in this town." Terry smiled before continuing. "I have started on my book, remember that?" It was Amy's turn to smile at this news.

"Regardless of how things go, I'm here to stay on the Coast." Terry didn't say it, but they both knew he was talking about their relationship. He then changed the subject. "What about you? What have you been doing since you came to the Coast?"

"I found a nursing position at Greymouth Hospital. They were very good when I had the children.

16

They gave me time off and allowing me to have shifts that suited the family. I am still there and will probably stay till I retire."

"You are on days off?"

"No. I am on a month's leave now. They wanted me to have the leave when Brett and Michael had the accident, but I needed to keep busy then, so am taking the time now." Amy paused before continuing "Lucy is sitting her final school exams. I'm really happy that she may be following me into nursing."

"Perhaps you can show me around the local sights while you are on leave?' Terry asked with a quizzical smile. "What are you doing on the Weekend?"

Amy had to think quickly. She would have to change her plans to stay out at the bach for the whole weekend.

"I'm free Saturday morning. Can I take you for a drive up to Punakaiki and have some lunch?"

"Sounds good. What do you usually do on the weekends, or are you working?"

"Sometimes I do if I am needed." Amy didn't tell Terry she was able choose the days and the hours she worked. She realised though, that he was going to be a regular part of her life, whether she was ready for him to be in it or not.

"I often go out to the family bach at the lake for the weekend. I will take you out some time."

"I will look forward to it." They parted with her promise to collect Terry at 10 o'clock. "What if it is raining?"

"Bring your umbrella and a plastic cover for your clothes. Do you have gum boots? If not, you will need to get some!" she added with a grin.

"We will go for a run up to Greymouth for lunch instead and have a detour to Lake Brunner and Mitchells on the way home."

Terry realised he needed to do some shopping! He had brought his umbrella with him, which he had used occasionally since he came, for his walks around the town and along the beach when it wasn't too windy. A raincoat and gum boots was something he hadn't needed till now. Terry had a feeling he would be introduced to places where he would be needing them.

"How was your lunch?" Lucy wanted to know when her mother returned. Whatever feelings her mother had for Terry; she was keeping them to herself for now. She looked as though she had just popped out for some groceries instead of having a reunion with her ex-husband. Lucy was both interested and anxious to know how her mother felt about him. Lucy was acutely aware that this man could have been her father if circumstances had been different. She was anxious to know whether her mother was developing a relationship with him again and how it would impact on their relationship.

Amy sensed that Lucy wanted to know how things stood between her and Terry. "It was very pleasant." Amy began. "Terry is here to stay on the Coast and has rented a house to live in for now. He is planning to write a book, something he wanted to do years ago, but never got around to. He has asked me to show him the sights around here while I am on holiday." Amy paused. "I am taking him up to Punakaiki tomorrow for lunch, or to Greymouth and a run to Lake Brunner on the way back if it is wet."

"We aren't going out to the bach this weekend then?"

Amy smiled. "Yes, we are going out and having dinner with your Nanna and Grandad as usual and staying out there. I will just be away for lunch tomorrow, but will be back for tea. You can make some ham and cheese toasties for us in the fire. Sunday will be for whatever you want to do out there."

"Oh good!" Lucy loved making toasties in the fire. She was also happy that most of the weekend would be how they had planned it.

"Lucy," Amy looked at her daughter with both loving and anxious eyes. "It is very early in my relationship with Terry. I am not in a rush to begin or restart anything. At the moment we are just getting to know each other again. It is 17 years since we parted. I will let you know if there are any developments in our relationship."

Just then, the home phone rang. Lucy pounced on it, knowing that Hoani or one of her other friends were on the other end.

"I will just ask." was the response Amy heard from the kitchen as she packed up the food they would need for the weekend.

"Mum, can Reka and Hoani and the gang come out too?"

"Tell them to be here for four o'clock."

Amy smiled. This meant they would have a full house out at the bach for the weekend, but she didn't mind. They were a happy bunch, and would keep Amy occupied while she was out for lunch. Brett's parents would be there too, to keep an eye on the young ones.

As dinner was served at the bach, there was a roar as rain poured down outside.

The lights flickered as the rumble of thunder rolled around the lake hills. Amy quickly grabbed the candles from the kitchen cupboard, just in case they had to spend the remainder of the evening without power.

After dinner, Amy settled down on the sofa by the fire with Myrtle and Frank while Lucy and her friends were playing cards at the table by candle light. Lizzie their Labrador stretched herself out on the rug in front of them.

"How did your lunch go?" Myrtle had been very patient and waited till dinner was over before broaching the subject.

Amy's expression was thoughtful. "It was quite interesting. Terry acknowledged that he put his job before our relationship. None of his friendships have come to anything, as they were like me. They weren't prepared to put up with him putting his job before their relationship either. He is also here to stay." Amy nodded as Myrtle raised her eyebrows at this news.

"Management at the bank have called for redundancies for managers in his position, so he has taken one. He has started to write a book while he is deciding what he will do next."

"Where is he staying now?" Frank wanted to know. "Not still at the hotel?"

"No. He is renting Molly's old house up Revell Street. I will be interesting to see if her family have spruced it up at all since she passed away." Amy paused. "I may be seeing it tomorrow. Terry asked me to show him some of the sights on the Coast while I am on holiday. If it is fine tomorrow, I will be taking him up to Punakaiki for lunch. I will be back for tea."

"What if It's wet like this?" Frank asked with a grin.

Amy answered his grin. "I will take him to Grey for lunch and come back via Brunner and Mitchells."

"Will you be bringing him back here afterwards?"

"No. Not this time. We are getting to know each other again. It is too early yet to know whether our relationship will develop again." Amy gave a sigh. " I would be quite happy if we stay just as friends."

Myrtle was firm. "Then you need to tell him that sooner than later, in case he is hoping that he can carry on where he left off."

Amy gave Myrtle a grateful smile. She could always be relied upon to give good advice. "Thank you Myrtle, I will."

When Amy collected Terry the next morning, the rain had passed, though the skies remained grey. Terry had a backpack with him.

"Do you think we will need these?" Terry asked as he came to the car.

"Pop them in the back. You never know. You may need them later."

"How is Molly's house?" Amy asked in conversation as they pulled away.

"Do you want to see inside?" Terry asked more keenly than he intended to sound. He knew he had to take things slowly if he wanted to be a part of her life again.

"Not particularly." Amy was cursing herself for asking and hoped he didn't take it that she wanted to restoke their relationship already. Keeping her voice casual, Amy continued. "I remember it was very rundown when Molly was living there. I'm just interested to know whether her family have done it up at all for the rental."

She gave him a grin. "If it hasn't been, then it should be dirt cheap!"

Terry answered her grin. "It's dirt cheap! Though it does have a shabby charm." He thought of the clean lines of his flat where nothing was out of place. It seemed almost too sterile now. He was glad he had put it on the market now.

"Are you allowed to do anything to it?" Amy wanted to know, like painting or putting up any pictures?"

"Actually I'm waiting to hear if they will sell it to me. It looks a complete wreck, but it is basically sound with some nice features that should be saved. In the meantime, I have hot water. The loo and cooker both work along with the old fridge. I have the added bonus of seeing the sunset from the Kitchen. I can walk through to the beach from the back gate; and I get to sleep to the sound of the ocean!" Terry ended on that note of triumph.

Amy laughed. "It isn't taking much to make you happy here."

"You're right." Terry replied more seriously. "My priorities in life have completely changed since I came here, and I'm glad of it."

As they made their way up the coast, the conversation flowed about general things they now liked to do, something they had rarely done while in their relationship. Amy now realised what a wasted time they had together and was glad that part of their life had ended when it did. Terry seemed to read her thoughts.

"We hardly ever did this while we were together, did we?" Terry spoke with regret. "What a waste of our lives!"

"It wasn't completely wasted." Amy spoke slowly as she articulated her thoughts. "We did find out what our priorities were, which were for different things at the time." Amy took a deep breath before she continued.

"I'm not sure what your intentions are for our relationship, but I need you to know, that I still love Brett. It is going to take some time to learn to live without him. The only thing I can give you is my friendship."

"Thank you for your honesty. I'm just glad that you think we can be friends." Terry paused. "That calls for a celebration ,I think!"

Amy raised her eyebrows. She gave him a brief glance as she negotiated the bends at Ten mile.

"What are we celebrating?"

"Our friendship!" Terry grinned.

After that Terry was quiet as he enjoyed the views of the coastal road and the canopy of the bushland covering the Paparoa ranges as it sloped down to the sea. Waves were sweeping in to the bays and coves along the coast, showering the green hillsides with their spray.

Amy saw the waves and made the comment. "It should be putting on a good show for us today."

"What show?"

Amy grinned. "You will see when we get there."

Once parked, Terry noticed big stands of palms he had never seen before.

"They are Nikau Palms, and are common in this area." Amy informed him.

Across the road Amy led Terry through a path that was heavily covered in a bushland tunnel before coming out into the open with large areas of flax and grey flat stones which were stacked on each other like pancakes.

Terry had heard the sound of waves crashing and now he saw it! Coming up through the blowholes in the rocks was an enormous spray of water that soaked anyone that was too close to it.

Amy pulled her camera out of her bag to take some photos, including one of Terry by the spray. A couple nearby asked her to take a photo of them with the spray, which she did. They then offered to take one of them. Terry quickly pulled his phone out to give it to them. Amy was feeling so self-conscious at having Terry's arm around her again, she wasn't sure she had smiled. He seemed happy with the photo, so she didn't press him for a look.

Terry loved the wild beauty of the rocks. When it came time to leave, he commented. "We will have to come again some time."

Amy nodded. "Her mood is different every time I come. You were lucky to see the blowholes this time. They are usually empty when the sea is calm."

At lunch in Greymouth, Terry insisted on a glass of wine with it.

"To us" Terry made his toast.

"To our friendship" Amy made her toast.

When Amy dropped Terry off, he wanted to know when their next outing was going to be.

"I'm busy tomorrow and Monday. We will have a day out on Tuesday. I will see you at nine."

"No clues where we are going?"

"It will be a surprise. By the way, can you ride a bike?"

Terry looked alarmed at this idea.

"Obviously not! We will have to teach you."

"Is this a bike tour?"

"No. That's for the future."

Once inside, Terry allowed himself a big smile. He was back in Amy's life, and he had no intention of leaving it. He looked at the photo of them together at Punakaiki. A look of doubt was still in her eyes.

"I won't let you down this time."

That evening a knock came at the door. It was Molly's grandson and the local lawyer who had a briefcase in his hand. They were here to negotiate the sale of the house.

Back at the bach, Myrtle Frank and Lucy awaited Amy's arrival with interest.

"How did it go?"

"We had another pleasant outing." Amy kept her voice casual. "The blowholes were performing well and we had a leisurely lunch at Greymouth on the way back."

"You don't have anything else planned?"

"Yes. I'm taking him out for the day on Tuesday."

"It's a pity I have exams, or I would come with you. Where are you going?"

"Down to Franz Joseph for lunch and have a walk."

"You aren't going up on the Glacier?" Frank asked.

Amy looked thoughtful as she considered it. "It depends on what the weather is like. There is no use in getting a flight up there if the cloud is down or it's raining."

"Do you mind if we tag along too?" Myrtle asked.

"Not at all." Amy grinned. "The more people that come, the merrier!"

"Make sure you bring your bathers!" Myrtle told her.

"Bathers?"

"Haven't you tried the hot springs yet?"

"I'm not sure Terry has a pair, or if he does, whether he has them with him."

"I will bring a spare pair, just in case." Frank twinkled at her.

I'm really jealous I'm missing out!" Lucy complained. "Can't you do this when we all can come?" The look of expectation on the faces of Lucy and her friends made Amy realise she had to change her plans.

"Alright then, we will go the week after next when your exams are finished."

"What's your plan B for Tuesday?" Myrtle asked with a chuckle, now that Amy's plans had been railroaded.

"I'm thinking of driving to Mitchells for a walk along the boardwalk and in to the Carew falls, then on to Moana for lunch. There is a walk along that side as well."

Myrtle nodded. "You will be running out of places to take him."

"Not at all!" Amy grinned. "There are the Coal Creek falls, the Gorge and the Skywalk. Lake Mahinapua has several walks and of course there is the cycleway when Terry has learnt to ride."

Myrtle didn't mention it, but Amy's plan to teach Terry to ride and take cycle rides in the future, showed that Terry was becoming a part of Amy's life, and they needed to adjust to having him in the family. She just wondered how Lucy was going to react to him joining the family.

# PLANNING FOR THE FUTURE

Amy pulled up outside Terry's house. There was no sign of him, so she turned off the motor and walked up to the front door and knocked. She noticed that the front garden was tidier that when she dropped Terry off last time. Terry opened the door with a grin. The smell of fresh paint assailed her.

"Come in and see the changes!"

Amy admired the bright daffodil yellow adorning the walls of the hallway, which ran through the centre of the house to the kitchen. White contrast now adorned the archway which gave a hint of grandeur of previous times.

"You have been busy! They are allowing you to do it up?"

"No. I've bought it." Terry replied with a satisfied smile.

The Lounge room had the floor stripped back to the floor boards. Tins of varnish and paint were waiting to restore the floor and walls. Amy saw the burgundy chrysanthemums on the tiles on the fireplace surround and wondered what colour would be painted in this room.

"It's going to be burgundy with white picture rails." Terry spoke, reading her thoughts.

The front bedroom opposite had a floral pattern feature wall behind the bed. The other walls were co-ordinated with duck-egg blue paint. Amy was envious of the wardrobe which had flowers in the stained glass window in the door.

"You need another wardrobe in here," Amy commented. "for his and hers."

"I will do." Terry replied, "when "she" joins me." with a grin on his face.

Amy turned away, trying to hide her embarrassment. She needed to think before she made comments that would encourage him! Down the hall, all the old wallpaper had been removed from the wall of the second bedroom. Rolls of wallpaper and pots of paint sat in the middle of the room, ready for its restoration. Also piles of white tiles were waiting to line the walls of the bathroom across the hall. Federation green tiles were also ready to line the shower cubicle. Amy also admired the old dresser with mirror, which had been transformed into a vanity and the new toilet unit, both waiting to be plumbed in. Across the hall, the bathroom floor was still covered in layers of old lino.

"Look at this!" Terry spoke as he lifted a section of the lino near the doorway. Underneath he revealed the original Federation green and white tiles, still in excellent condition.

The kitchen, when they entered, was a complete contrast. Dark, dingy and grotty walls greeted them. The old fridge, sat next to a small trough at one end. Amy could see the concrete slab where the copper used to be for washing clothes. An antique gas stove hugged the wall next to a home built cupboard with a sink. A small Formica table and two chairs sat under the window that looked out the back towards the ocean.

"I have plans for it." Terry reassured Amy, seeing her look of horror at the dismal scene. "I am getting plans drawn up for council approval to completely renovate and extend it."

"I'm glad to hear it!" Amy exclaimed, as she turned to lead Terry out.

Terry was disappointed she didn't stay to hear what his plans for the Kitchen and new living area and back yard of the section were, but he comforted himself that she would get an even bigger surprise when that area was transformed.

"You know you've missed your calling!" Amy said as they walked out to the car.

At Terry's enquiring look, she explained. "You have a natural flair for interior decorating. You could do worse than take it up as a business."

"Hmmm. It's something to think about." Terry tried to sound casual, but he was secretly thrilled that she liked what he was doing so much.

"Where are we heading today?" Terry was interested to know as they headed towards the northern end of the town.

Just then, Terry's phone rang. "Sorry." Terry said as he answered it. After listening to the message, Terry replied. "It's a cash sale? That's great news – and they want the furniture? I can catch the afternoon plane up and get it settled in the morning."

At Terry's words, Amy turned the car around at the next corner and headed for the travel office.

"Thanks." Terry said as he realised where Amy was now heading. "I've had an offer on the unit in Auckland, so I have to go up to do the paperwork."

"That's good news! You were asking where we are going." Amy replied. "I had intended to go south, but the family insisted that trip wait untill they can come with us the week after next when Lucy has finished her exams.

My plan B was for a trip to lake Brunner, but you will need to get back earlier for your flight, so a visit to the skywalk at Lake Mahinapua and some lunch at the café there is a better option."

Terry grinned at the prospect of having the family join them for their outing. "What's so special down south?"

"We are going down to Franz Joseph Glacier. It is a very scenic trip down to it. There is a chance we will be going for a helicopter ride, and bring your bathers!"

"How many of us will be going?" Terry asked, making a mental note to buy some bathers and a towel. Swimming wasn't something he had bothered with in his previous life!

Amy had to think for a minute. "Well Frank and Myrtle are coming, and Lucy will be bringing three or four of her friends. We will probably be in Franks van. We can get about eight or nine in there."

"You are lucky!" Maureen the travel agent commented when she booked Terry's flight. "You have the last seat. Do you want to book a return flight?"

Terry hesitated as he thought of all the things he had to sort in his flat. It was going to take a day or two to decide whether to give things away or bring them back with him. He already suspected there was too much to bring back on a flight.

"Thanks, but I will book it from the other end if I decide to fly back. I suspect I will have to hire a large vehicle and drive back – I have a flat to sort and bring some of it back." Both Amy and Maureen grinned at the idea of Terry being swamped under a van load of his possessions.

Maureen looked at Amy with interest. Everyone knew she had just buried her husband and son and wondered how she had met Terry so soon afterwards. Amy saw the look and felt the need to explain.

"Terry is my ex-husband. We parted before I met Brett. We are now friends. He very kindly came to help me get through the funeral."

"And I'm here to stay." Terry announced to the room. He picked up his ticket, giving Amy a cheeky smile. "Are we still going for that Sky Walk and lunch?"

"We are." Amy smiled and tried to be nonchalant as she stood up to lead him out of the office.

"Enjoy you too!" Maureen called after them. Amy had no doubt that their relationship would soon be the subject of talk around the town.

When Terry boarded the plane that afternoon, his thoughts were of Amy and his home here, instead of the task that lay ahead of him in Auckland. Amy had been more relaxed as they climbed the walkways that lead to the tower in the treetops, with 360 degree views across the lake to the ocean in the west, round to the Alps in the east. For once there was no cloud to hide their jagged snow-capped peaks standing out against the blue of the sky.

Over their lunch, Amy asked the question which had been teasing her since she saw the changes to Terry's house.

"What are your plans for the kitchen and out back?"

Terry tried to hide his happiness that she was interested in his plans for the house by reaching for a serviette. Amy also reached for a biro from her bag to give him.

After making a rough plan of the current house on the paper, he then outlined the changes to the kitchen.

"A laundry here."

"and perhaps a toilet off it for guests?" Amy suggested. "Most people prefer to keep their bathroom private. You could put some storage in that space next to it." Terry nodded at her suggestion and pencilled it in. He couldn't help a smile that she was getting involved in the plans. They spent time discussing the placement of a new kitchen that would fit the current space. "We will put a steel in here." Terry indicated where the back wall currently was. "and open the area up for a dining and family area. We will extend the roof through, but have a bank of windows on the three sides with doors out on the sheltered side. What sort of windows would you like in there?" "Actually, I've seen some lovely windows at the antique yard down the wharf end of Revell Street. They have plain glass and can open at the bottom, but have stained glass at the top. I wonder if they are still there?""Shall we have a look when we've finished this? Amy nodded her agreement. She then looked at the plan again.

"That second bedroom is much bigger than the front one. I'm just wondering if we could pinch some of the space for an ensuite and walk in wardrobe. That lovely wardrobe would be placed in the second bedroom for guests along with a couch that converts to a bed. You could have that room for your office. There is room for a desk at the window, with cupboards and shelves next to it for your business files."

"I like the idea of an office." Terry agreed. "What about you? You don't want or need an area for hobbies or books?"

"I could do with a desk and cupboard for my sewing machine and materials. Would there be room in there for it? I do have some books. Perhaps we could have a bookshelf or make a library in the front room?"

"I have a collection of books I want to keep too, so making a library in the front room makes sense. I might make an upstairs area for our office and craft area though, that has a nice view of the sea."

"We've done it, haven't we?" Amy commented on returning to the car.

Terry looked at her with a quizzical look.

"We've rebonded."

"Yes we have." Terry agreed. Giving her hand a squeeze.

When they visited the antique yard, Terry was stunned at the variety and beauty of the windows on offer. A number of windows were put aside for Amy to collect later, as it was now time for Terry to collect his bag and head for the airport.

"I will be away for at least a week. I'm on the lookout for some furniture and fittings while I'm up there and will send some photos for your approval."

"It sounds like you will need a separate truck when you come back!" Amy grinned.

The kiss Terry gave Amy as he prepared to leave, was with a tenderness he had never displayed before.

Back home, both Lucy and her neighbour Claire were waiting with interest for a report on her day out.

"It has been an interesting day." Amy couldn't hide a little smile as she said it. That smile told both Lucy and Claire that Amy had rekindled her relationship with Terry.

"Terry has bought Molly's cottage and is doing it up. He has sold his unit in Auckland and is on his way up there as I speak."

"How was your day at Lake Brunner?" Lucy wanted to know.

"We didn't get there today. Terry showed me what he had done to Molly's house so far and what he is planning to do to it. We set out for Brunner, but the call came through about his unit, so we made a detour to the travel agent. It was too late by then to go to Brunner, so we did the Sky walk and had lunch at the café. We also paid a visit to the antique yard for some windows before he left."

"When is he due back?" Lucy wanted to know.

"Terry will be away for at least a week. He will be doing some shopping for the house while he is up there."

"You aren't having any input?" Claire enquired.

"Of course! He is sending me photos for my approval."

"I would like to see what Terry has done." Claire commented. "It was pretty run down, as I remember, when Molly lived there."

"I would like to see it too." Lucy joined in. "She wasn't going to miss seeing the place where her mother would be living.

"Are you free tomorrow afternoon Claire?"

"I finish at two."

"My exam finishes by lunch time." Lucy added.

"We will collect you at 2.30 Claire."

In the morning Amy collected the windows. Feeling restless, Amy put down some cloths to protect the lounge room floor and started to paint the first wall in the lounge room.

The long arm of the roller soon covered a big area. By the time Lucy had finished her exam, only the picture rails and the varnish on the floor needed to be done.

Both Claire and Lucy were impressed with the plans for the home and the renovations that had been done so far. Lucy was also pensive.

"When are you moving in Mum, and what are you going to do with our house?"

Amy gave Lucy a reassuring smile. "I will move in when you are ready to take over the Kaniere road house."

When Terry sent her some photos that evening, Amy also had some to send him.

During the next week, the lino in the bathroom made its way to the tip, and a visit was made by the tiler to tile the bathroom walls. The plumber also came to install the bathroom furniture. During the visit to the antique yard, Amy had spotted a roll-topped bath in good condition, which made its way into the bathroom. A coat of Federation green now adorned its outer shell.

During the week, the council building inspector also came for a visit after plans for the extension had been emailed to him. He toured the front of the house in silence, surprised at its good condition. It was only when he came through to the kitchen that he began to have doubts.

"Has a survey been done of the house?" he wanted to know.

"Yes. Terry had one done before he made an offer for the house. Do you want a copy sent to you?"

"Yes please."

"The stumps under the front of the house are sound, and all the stumps in the kitchen are to be redone with the extension. The electrics are to be redone and the plumber has prepared the pipes for when the mains come through next year."

"Where are all those windows in the spare room going?"

"They are for the bank of windows in the family room extension" Amy showed the inspector on the plan he had brought with him.

"I'm not sure they will last long in the winter gales we have here." The inspector was doubtful.

"We plan to install external roller shutters to protect them in any gales we may have."

"Do you have plans for anything else either attached or separate to the house?"

"We may erect a car port at the front and a Pagola in the back garden."

"We will want plans for those. If separate, they are to be a metre from both the building and either fence or boundary line. I'm happy to sign off on these plans, though they will still have to have final approval by the council."

"Thank you."

"I will be back to see how things are progressing."

"We will look forward to showing you the transformation."

In Auckland, Terry was approaching the manager of a large plant nursery. He had noticed that most of their plants were not native.

"I am moving to Westland and intend to set up a plant nursery for native plants and trees. Do you have a market for them?"

The manager's eyes lit up.   She swiftly gave Terry her card. "Call me as soon as you have plants available."

# TERRY RETURNS

Amy was admiring her handywork in the front lounge. The Ceiling, and picture rails had a new coat of white paint, which contrasted well with the burgundy on the walls. The floor also displayed a sheen from the coats of varnish she had applied. She looked at the windows. The old net curtains needed to go! Amy was measuring the window to estimate how much material she needed for new curtains, when a large RV and a truck pulled up outside. Terry was back! When she ventured outside to meet Terry, Amy was greeted with a big hug and a kiss that made her blush! She wondered whether the neighbours had seen it!

"Come and see the changes." Amy smiled as she led Terry and the delivery driver and his mate up the path.

"It looks even better than I envisioned it!" Terry gave Amy another hug as he looked at the front lounge and the now complete bathroom.

Once the furniture was installed in the lounge, juggling had to be done to find room for the kitchen units and appliances which filled up much of the second bedroom. The windows for the family room ended up in the front bedroom and the couch for the second bedroom and desks for the office had to find a home in the lounge for the time being.

"Where are we going to put the rest of it?" the driver wanted to know.

Terry and Amy followed him out to the truck to see what else needed a home. Laundry appliances, a dining set and furniture for the family area were there.

Amy smiled when she saw a bike and helmet among the items. He had remembered her promise to teach him to ride!

"Perhaps it can go in the shed?" Amy suggested. "it will need to be out of the way untill the back is done."

"Are you sure?" Terry asked.

"I'm sure." Amy agreed. "You will need to live out with us while the renovations are going on anyway. You won't get much peace while that is happening and you won't have any cooking facilities either."

After showing the driver where they were to go on the map, a small convoy followed Amy out Kaniere Road to her house.

Lucy was relaxing on the verandah, now her exams were finally over, when she heard vehicles coming up the drive. Her mother's car was in front with another bigger vehicle behind and a big truck at the back. She realised that Terry was here to stay, and was entertained for the next couple hours as the truck contents were transferred to the shed and Terry emptied the contents of the RV; most of it to the shed and the rest of it indoors. The driver and his mate happily accepted drinks and lunch which was served for everyone out on the verandah, before they set off on the long drive back to Auckland.

Lucy eyed Terry's bike with interest. She would enjoy showing him the old Tram track which passed their property.

"I will have to return the RV to Christchurch tomorrow." Terry mentioned to Amy.

"We will bring the car over and drive you back." Amy smiled. "If we make an early start, we should be back for tea."

"Will there be time for some shopping?" Lucy asked hopefully.

"We will be having some lunch over there. Will a stop at the Riccarton Mall be sufficient, or do you want go in the city centre?"

"I was hoping to look in the central malls."

"We will see how time goes. Can you be up and ready to go for seven?"

"Can you wake me at six?"

"I can."

Terry and Amy exchanged smiles. Negotiating with teenagers was something he had to get used to.

"Will we be going out to the bach, when we come back?" Lucy asked. "Should we pack a bag for the weekend, so we can go straight out when we return?"

"That's a good idea! I will take Lizzie and our food for the weekend over to Claire and get her to take them out, as she will be ready to go out before us."

When Terry brought his belongings into Amy's house, he noticed that there were two bedrooms in the house. The third room was given over to craft and painting. A magnificent painting of a Tui feeding on Kaka Beak was sitting on an easel. Terry was staring at the easel, wondering who had done it, when he heard movement behind him. He looked around to find Lucy looking at him with a cheeky smile.

"Do you like it?"

"You did this? It's wonderful! What will you be doing with it?"

"We will find a spot for it somewhere."

"Well, if you don't, I would like to buy it from you for my house, and if you have any others, I would like to see them too!"

At Lucy's shocked look, Terry asked "You haven't sold any before?" When she shook her head, "Well, look on it as your first commission."

"Where will you be putting it?" Lucy wanted to know.

"It will have pride of place over the fireplace in the front room." Terry took another look at the painting. "You haven't finished it yet!"

"What have I missed?" Lucy asked with alarm, that he had spotted something that wasn't quite right.

"Your signature and date is missing!"

"That's easily fixed." Lucy sighed with relief. Picking up a brush with some black paint and quickly initialled and dated it in the bottom corner.

Hearing their voices, Amy came to see what was happening, and was surprised to find them discussing Lucy's latest painting. She had been wondering where she was going to put it, but the beam on Lucy's face told her that issue had been solved.

"Mum! Terry has just bought my painting, and he wants to see my others as well!"

"That will be nice pocket money for you." Amy commented, glad that Lucy wouldn't be looking for any from her for a little while. When Terry mentioned the amount he wanted to pay her for it, both Lucy and Amy looked at him in shock.

"That's going straight into a bank account for you." Amy spoke firmly.

Lucy nodded. "I will get the others out later for you to see." She was still reeling from the surprise that someone valued them so much.

Amy saw the bags Terry had in his hands. "Bring those through to our room."

Terry followed Amy into a big bright room. A colourful quilt covered the bed and warm rugs were scattered on the wooden floor. She opened the wardrobe door.

"You can put your things this end and use the drawers on your side." Amy smiled as she turned to leave him to unpack.

Instead Terry put down the bags and took her into his arms and held her close for several minutes. When he released her, Terry noticed that Amy had tears in her eyes.

"What's the matter?" he asked softly.

"Nothing's wrong. I'm just not used to this gentle treatment!" Amy managed a smile.

Terry grinned. "Then it's time you got used to it!" and brushed a feather like kiss onto her lips before the kiss deepened. When they parted, Amy's pulse was pounding. He turned to bring more of his possessions from the RV. After Terry left the house, Lucy came in to the room and gave her mother a searching look.

"Was he like this before?"

"No, he wasn't." Amy smiled, realising that Lucy had witnessed their embrace.

"I'm glad it's going to be better for you this time. I just hope my partner is as considerate when the time comes."

Terry was pleased the roads were quiet as they set out on their journey across the Alps. Their tops were covered in early morning cloud. Once they started to negotiate the steep and winding road through from Otira to Arthur's Pass, Terry found he had to concentrate on the road, instead of allowing his eyes to be drawn to the soaring peaks around them. He was looking forward to having a proper look at them on the way back.

They stopped at Arthur's Pass township. Their cars were immediately surrounded by the local Keas who showed a keen interest in their tyres and the rubber trims on their car windows, untill they were shooed away. Back on the road, Terry also marvelled at the reflection of the surrounding mountains on Lake Pearson and the shapes of the rocks standing on Castle Hill. He vowed to come back for a proper visit one day. Terry was surprised at how dry, but fertile the Canterbury plain was as they passed numerous farms on the way into the city, many of the paddocks were bordered by tall poplar and fir trees.

Once the RV was dropped off, Lucy was happy to be taken into the central city where they had a browse around the malls and some lunch. Terry found he was helping to carry some of Lucy's "bargains" back to the car.

"Don't you have any shops at home?" Terry asked with some bemusement.

"We do." Lucy smiled tolerantly at Terry's expression of amazement, but we don't have the variety and the prices are better here."

On the way back through the pass, both Amy and Lucy were surprised at the number of times Terry made the comment, "We will have to make time for a stop here, next time." Over the years they had become accustomed to the scenery, which they gave a passing glance on the way through.

"Do we have any plant nurseries on the Coast?" Terry asked Amy after they passed Kumara junction and the Tasman Sea came into view for the first time. This question gave both Amy and Lucy food for thought. They were silent for a minute or two as they considered his question.

43

"They sell some plants for gardens in the supermarket." Lucy offered.

"I think the council has a nursery." Amy commented.

"Do they sell plants to the public?"

"No, I don't think they do."

"Do they sell native plants in the supermarket?"

"No. We go for a walk in the bush when we want to be in nature, why?"

"Would you consider having native trees and plants in your garden if they were available?"

Both Amy and Lucy were wondering where this line of questioning was heading, when the penny dropped!

"You're going to start a native plant nursery?"

Terry nodded and smiled. "I have arranged to supply a large nursery in Auckland. "I'm just wondering whether there would be any interest locally as well."

"That's wonderful news!" Amy beamed.

"My next step is to look at buying or leasing some land and put some green houses on them for planting and growing seedlings till they have grown strong enough to be outside."

Lucy looked at her mother. "We've got plenty of land for a project like this!" She then stunned them with her next statement. "We have Mum looking after people, I will be looking after animals and Terry caring for plants, I think this family has got everything covered!"

"What will your job be, looking after animals?" Terry wanted to know, seeing the stunned expression on Amy's face.

Lucy smiled. "Depending on my results, I will train to be a vet, specialising in wildlife. I will be approaching the vet here for some experience while in training and hopefully get a position here with them afterwards. If I don't, I will look at being a vet nurse. I will also be a carer for animals on the side. We have a large shed that is under-utilised, that can be used for animals that need to be indoors and a paddock next to it for animals that are ready for rehabilitation outside."

"You have got it all worked out already. I'm impressed!"

Amy suppressed the disappointment that Lucy wouldn't be following her into nursing. It was obvious that Lucy had found her passion for caring for animals. She would do what she could to help her achieve it! Both Amy and Terry were delighted that Lucy not only accepted Terry into the household, but she also considered them to be a family now.

As Amy's car approached Hokitika, after their trip to Christchurch, Terry's phone rang. It was Rick the builder. "I've been trying to get you. The council has approved your renovation. Can I see you this evening to go over the details?"

Terry looked at Amy, who could hear the conversation.

"We are on our way out to Amy's bach at Lake Kaniere. Can we meet tomorrow?"

"Is that Myrtle and Frank's family bach?"

"It is." Amy spoke quietly.

"Yes, it is." Terry confirmed.

"I will see you in a few of hours. We have a bach out there too. By the way, you will have to go to Kaniere via Arthurs Town. There's been an accident out Kaniere road. All traffic is being diverted."

"What about the Blue Spur Road?" Amy asked.

"No, don't try to go out that way." Rick answered Amy's question. "They are only allowing traffic coming from Kaniere to use that road."

Amy joined the line of traffic that were all heading for the bridge.

"It's just as well we have the bach." Amy commented, "Otherwise we all would be staying at the hotel for the night." She paused as a thought came to her mind. "I wonder how many others can't get home tonight?"

Her question was soon answered by the ring of her phone, which was in her bag. Lucy dived into her mother's bag to answer it.

"Is that you Lucy?" It was Hoani and Reka and their friends Micky and Kelly. Their families lived along the Kaniere Road from Amy and Lucy's home. "Where are you?"

"We are queueing for the bridge to go out to the bach. Why?"

"Can you take us with you? We can't get home. We are near the bridge."

"I will tell her."

"Mum, Hoani and the gang need a lift. They can't get home. They are by the bridge."

"I can see them." Amy responded. She saw Terry's shocked expression when they piled into the car, Reka and Kelly sat on Hoani and Micky's knees.

"We are going to have a full house again this weekend. You could say they are our extended family."

"Do your parents know you are coming out?" Terry wanted to know.

Hoani gave him a grin. "Not yet. Why?"

"If I was your parent, I would want to know where you were and that you were okay."

With a mock sigh, Hoani pulled out his phone and made the call. Both Terry and Amy could hear the concern in the raised voice of his father Hori on the other end, demanding to know where he was. It took reassurances from Terry and Amy, that Hoani and their friends were okay to stay with them at the bach before Hori calmed down.

"Is it okay for me and the missus to come out for a visit tomorrow afternoon?" Hori asked.

"We will look forward to it." Terry replied, looking at Amy with a grin. Once off the phone, he commented. "We will be packed to the rafters."

"Hopefully it will be fine and we can sit outside."
Amy grinned back. "Knowing Kohi, she will bring
enough food to feed an army and Hori will bring enough
liquid refreshments to quench a bar!"

When they came to the junction at Lake Kaniere,
Terry was given his first glimpses of the lake and the hills
surrounding it. He realised that he was coming to a
special place that would stay in his heart for ever.

Claire and her girls Linda and Megan were
waiting with Lizzie as the car pulled up at the bach.
Lizzie recognised the car and bounded down from the
front verandah to give everyone who exited the car a big
sloppy welcome.

Terry was surprised at how everyone mucked in
to help in the bach. Hoani and their friends lit the fire
and brought in enough wood to keep it going overnight.
Lucy, Reka and Claire's girls extended and set the table
while Claire and Amy started to prepare the meal for
everyone.

"Is there anything I can do?" Terry asked
hopefully.

"Can you go out to the garden and find a lettuce
and a couple of carrots?" Claire asked, pointing to a
sharp knife, for him to take.

Terry stepped outside and was struck by the cosy
feel in the back yard. It was surrounded by thick forest
which was inviting him in to explore. A dark green tin
shed was nestled next to the forest. A clematis vine
trailed over it. The roof was clothed in moss and lichen.
Next to the shed was the vegetable garden. Beyond it
were some fruit trees. A plum, pear and apple tree had
silver lichen covering their trunks and branches, though
the leaves and fruit that were forming looked healthy.

Terry looked up beyond the shed and bushland to feel the power of Tahua's steep slopes, as they rose behind the bach.

Terry heard the door open behind him. Hoani was coming out to join him.

"They sent me out to see if you got lost in the garden." Hoani joked with a smile.

"I was too busy admiring everything!" Terry replied looking at Tahua's slopes again.

"That's Mount Tahua. There's a nice view up the top."

"There is a track up there?"

"There is. I will take you some time."

"I will look forward to it." Terry smiled as he turned to find the lettuce and carrots in the garden. He managed to find a lettuce that wasn't eaten in its centre. The animals around here obviously helped themselves to the garden when the bach was empty. He left the outer leaves on the garden before handing it to Hoani, who smiled.

"No-one else does that." Hoani commented. "Leaving some for the animals."

"If anyone complains, its good compost for the garden."

Terry pulled the carrots and cut the tops off, leaving them on the garden.

"If you push the orange part into the soil, you will get another carrot to grow." Hoani informed him as he leant over to poke the carrot ends into the soil.

"You've just taught me something, thanks Hoani."

As they turned to walk inside, Hoani broach the subject that had been on his mind.

"Lucy mentioned you are starting a native plant nursery. Is there any chance of my getting some work with you when I'm home from Uni?"

"I'm sure I will find plenty for you to do." What course are you planning to do?

"I intend to do biology, though I'm torn between studying plants or animals." Hoani grinned. He spotted movement in the tree next to the shed. "It looks like Amy's animal family are here. They must be wanting some more books."

"What?" Terry was astonished. Where are they?"

"The Ruru and the Possum are in the tree above the shed. It's quite a story, but they have learnt to read books."

Terry looked over to the shed to find he was under the gaze of a Morepork Owl and a Possum that was hard to see as she had dark fur that blended in with the darkness of the foliage behind her. Only the pink around her nose and in her ears gave her presence away. Terry forced himself to keep moving towards the bach, even though he wanted to stay to watch them.

Inside, Amy accepted the vegetables gratefully and began to wash them under the tap.

"Your Ruru and Possum are here." Hoani told her.

"Are they?" Amy looked towards the door. "I haven't heard them!"

"They are in the tree by the shed."

Amy gave the lettuce and carrots to Claire, while she fetched a slate, chalk and an atlas of New Zealand and placed them by the back door. Just then, the sound of a car came into the drive. Terry went to the front door in case it was Rick, but it was Myrtle and Frank. He greeted them with a big smile.

"Come in Myrtle and Frank. Tea is being served."

"Nice to see you again." Myrtle spoke for both of them. Frank gave him a bottle of wine as he came in. Everyone was sitting themselves at the table as they came in. Another two settings were quickly put in place and Terry found some glasses for the wine. Terry noticed both Lucy and Hoani came over to give Myrtle and Frank a hug.

Terry found himself between Frank and Hoani at the table and managed to eat between fielding questions from Frank about how he had been settling in at Hokitika and questions from Hoani about his business plans. In a brief lull, Terry thought he heard scratching at the back door. He Looked over at Amy who was smiling at the attention he was getting from Frank and Hoani.

"I think your Owl and Possum are at the door." Terry told her.

The scratching at the door could be heard again.

Everyone at the table became quiet as they watched Amy collect the slate and map book and open the door, where she began to talk to the animals. Everyone was surprised when Amy fetched a roll of plastic contact and a glass of water and took them to the door. When Amy returned to the table, everyone looked at her with expectation.

"They want books for Fiordland this time." Amy announced. She looked at Terry before she continued. "Once the books are ready, we will be taking them down, and we will be taking Ogilvie with us."

"Who's Ogilvie?"

"Ogilvie is an Owl from Fiordland that is visiting the community here."

"You will be covering the books with contact?" Lucy asked.

"I will be." Amy confirmed. "It is very wet down there. I know the books won't last long without protection, so I showed Oriel and Peaches how the contact protects books from water. They were happy with it."

When Rick arrived to see Terry, he was surprised to see a full house at the bach.

'Would you like to come over to mine?" Rick offered.

"Good Idea." Terry agreed.

When Terry returned some hours later, the bach was quiet and dark except for a light in his and Amy's room. Claire and her girls had retreated to their bach. Frank and Myrtle were occupying the room that Lucy liked to use and the couches in the living area were set out as beds for Lucy's friends. An extra camp bed had been set up for Lucy with them. Amy was reading when he joined her in their room.

"Is it all sorted?" Amy asked with a smile.

Terry's answer was to drop a large pile of plans and detailed specifications onto her lap.

"They start on Monday." Terry grinned at her shocked expression.

"Will they need you to be around?"

"No. They can phone me if there are any issues and I will be popping in most days to keep an eye on things. He just wants me to put a lock on the connecting door from the kitchen to the front of the house. When do we go back to Kaniere Road house?"

"Sunday afternoon. We can do the lock then. By the way, we have a day out on Tuesday."

"Where are we heading this time?" Terry asked with interest.

"It's the family day down to the Glacier."

"What's wrong?" Amy asked at Terry's frown.

"I can't remember where I put my bathers and towel that I bought!"

"You have all Monday to find them. You should also keep a pair out here too!  It will soon be warm enough to swim in the lake here!"

As Terry cuddled up with Amy, he realised just how extensive Amy's "family" was.  She not only had Lucy and him to care for, Lucy's friends also considered her their second mother, and there was also the local animals that came to her as well.

When the time came to deliver the books to Fiordland, Terry was surprised at how smoothly it went.  They made a very early start in the morning, for a very long day.  Thanks to Amy's training of Ogilvie the owl the previous evening; teaching him to sit on and in a cage, which was now covered in towels and strapped to the back seat of their car.  He was no trouble, sitting on the cage till daylight came, then let himself into the cage to sleep for most of the day. Amy also had a supply of mice to feed Ogilvie, which he consumed during the trip.

Ogilvie announced their arrival at the meeting point by letting out an ear piercing call, almost deafening Terry and Amy and flapping his wings vigorously.  After being let out of the car, he joined Ocene, the owl leader of the Fiordland owl community.  They led Amy and Terry to into the forest to meet Teeny Tahr and  Kelan the Tokoeka leader of the Fiordland community.  Terry would never forget the sight of Teeny Tahr, who towered over him. His massive body reached Terry's shoulder.

Terry was just glad there weren't any deer stalkers around to see him, and that the Tahr obediently sat down when he saw the saddle that Amy carried with the carry bags attached. Terry also marvelled, that once they stepped away from loading the books, Kelan the Tokoeka Kiwi Leader at Fiordland immediately ran forward to climb onto Teeny's back, - as though he was used to having rides on animals. Afterwards Terry and Amy stopped at the Haast hotel for the night, and could only wonder about the final destination of the books they had just delivered.

# THE GLACIER TRIP

The Sky was clear with Mount Cook and Tasman's white and blue splendour standing out among the Southern Alps, as Frank joined the main highway south at Hokitika. Terry was sitting in the front with him, his bathers and towel were safely in a bag at his feet. Myrtle and Amy were sitting behind them with Lucy and her friends Kelly and Micky sitting behind them. Hori and Kohi were also following behind with Hoani and Reka in their car.

Hori and Kohi's visit to the Bach had been successful in more ways than one. As Amy had predicted, They had brought large baskets of both food and drink with them, resulting in a sumptuous meal in the evening after "grazing" in the afternoon. Hori's knowledge of cultivating plants from his job at the council nursery was passed on to Terry. Frank also listened in with interest. He hadn't broached the subject yet, but he also was interested in working in Terry's nursery.

Kohi shared Lucy's love of painting and the pair of them took their sketch pads out onto the verandah to do some sketching as everyone was sitting around chatting.

Hori had wondered why Hoani still spent much of his time over at Amy's after Michael had died, and now he knew. He wasn't overt about it, but it was obvious to Hori that Hoani was keen on Lucy, and one day they would be a couple. He would have to let the iwi at the Pa know about it, so they didn't try to pair Hoani with someone from the tribe.

Terry marvelled at the beauty of the forest at Ferguson's Bush, and the lakes that he only had a brief glimpse of as they sped by. He vowed to come back with Amy soon and have lots of stops at places he wanted to explore. At Whataroa they stopped at the Heron Sanctuary. Everyone loved the boat ride along the waterways, to see the Herons, their nests in the trees that lined the water's edge.

At the Franz Joseph township, they voted to have a swim in the hot pools before they had lunch. Terry had expected a normal pool complex, so when he was led along wooden walkways to numerous pools in a bush setting, some of which were private, he added this to another place to come back to with Amy. No-one wanted to get out when it was time to retreat for lunch. Lunch was a boisterous affair, with their party seeming to take over part of the café, with tables brought together for everyone to be together.

Afterwards, there was excitement as they drove to the Heliport for their ride to the glacier. It took some time to be weighed and sort who was flying with who. Frank, Myrtle and Lucy went together. Hori, Hoani and Micky took the next flight. Kohi, Reka and Kelly flew after them, with Terry and Amy going up last.

Terry was happy to be in the front with the pilot, as the helicopter rose above the treetops to fly up the valley, the top of the glacier glistening in the sunshine. A few wisps of cloud had formed in the mountains, but the winds were light. They couldn't have asked for a nicer day to come. Gaining height as they flew up the side of the glacier, Terry was grateful they didn't have to climb the terrain on the glacier, which was not only rough, but also many deep and treacherous crevasses.

There was relief that the area at the top of the glacier where they landed was flat and smooth. Everyone gathered together for a photo before the pilot left to pick up the next passengers waiting to visit. Frank and Myrtle, Hori and Kohi and Terry and Amy stood together talking and taking in the scene, with views not only of the surrounding mountains, but down the valley to the sea.

Lucy and her friends took a walk to the edge of the flat plateau at the top of the glacier. Before they could grab him, Hoani slipped on some ice and started to slide towards a crevasse. Despite his efforts to try to cling onto the side, Hoani disappeared out of sight. A scream told them that he had landed and hurt himself!

"HOANI!" Lucy screamed, knowing there was nothing she could do to help him. She turned round to shout to her mother, but both Terry and Hori were already running over as they had seen Hoani slip and disappear. Amy, Kohi and Frank and Myrtle weren't far behind.

"Come away from the side!" Hori ordered them as he and Terry arrived to see Lucy and Reka leaning over the edge. "We don't want anyone else in there!"

"Is he calling or talking since he fell?" Terry asked.

Lucy shook her head, her eyes full of misery. "We heard him scream when he fell in, but nothing since."

Just then Amy and the rest of the party came. Lucy went to her mother's arms for comfort, as did Reka to Kohi. Frank and Myrtle also came to give Micky and Kelly some comfort.

"Do we have the number of the Heliport?" Terry asked. The sooner emergency services are called, the better.

Amy was grateful she had brought her phone with her. She was also thankful that she had reception and was able to make contact. Once Amy explained the situation, she added. "I'm a nurse. Do you have a rope ladder and anchors handy so I can go down to assess how he is?"

"I will send them up with the next helicopter and am alerting emergency services."

It was only ten minutes before the sound of the helicopter's return, but it felt like much longer. A staff member, Dave who was also a member of the local rescue group, jumped out, bringing a large pack with him. He also had a satellite phone. As they showed him where Hoani had slid in, he shook his head at the slippery ice just under the surface.

"This may take a while, so most of you need to go back to the township. Also, if he has survived the fall, he will be airlifted straight over to Christchurch. The Nurse and one other person can go with him." Dave then opened the pack for the metal pegs and rope.

"If Hoani goes to Christchurch, we will see you there." Kohi managed to say in her anguish. Hori and Kohi had a brief cuddle to comfort each other, before Kohi took Reka, Kelly and Micky over to the helicopter. Frank and Myrtle came over to give Amy and Lucy a hug.

"Take care down there. If you go to Christchurch We will bring Lucy Reka and Kohi over."

"Thank you Frank." Amy was thankful for her nursing training to be able to be calm and focused for the task ahead and not think about the fact that one of her extended family was in dire trouble. "Can you call in and see Claire and let her know what is happening?"

"We will." Myrtle answered for them.

Terry also came to give Amy a hug. "Ring as soon as you have any news. I will probably have to stay in Hokitika to supervise the build, so I will look after Lizzie for you."

"Thank you Honey." Amy gave him a little smile, which was answered by Terry. "Honey" was her endearment for him during their previous relationship. They both looked around at Dave. The Hammering of the long metal pegs into the ice had stopped and he was attaching the rope ladder to them. It was almost time for her to descend. Terry gave Amy another cuddle and a firm kiss before he turned to join the rest of the party.

"Put these on." Dave instructed Amy as he passed her a lightweight suit that covered her whole body; to put on over her clothes. "We don't want you getting hypothermia down there too." Dave was putting a suit on too.

"I will go down first." Dave instructed Amy. "I will call "Okay" when I'm down. If the ladder breaks, just wait for the rest of the team to come."

"Has that happened before?" Amy was astonished.

"Not to me, but it has happened to others." Dave answered as he repacked the pack, and slung it over his shoulders before stepping onto the ladder. Amy took particular notice how he placed his hands and feet, as she knew it would be different to using an ordinary ladder. As the helicopter rotated and lifted into the air, Amy gave it a little wave, before turning to listen for Dave's call. She was feeling warm in the suit, but knew she would need it down in the glacier. Amy was admiring the change from the white colour of the surface, to light then dark blue down below when Dave's call came.

"Okay you can come down now."

"I'm coming." Amy called back.

Remembering how Dave placed his hands and feet, Amy followed him down. She had to stop for a few seconds when she entered the crevasse. The ladder was no longer resting on the ice and started to swing. Dave grabbed the swing to steady it for Amy, so she was able to manage the rest of the climb down without incident.

The dark blue of the ice here made the area darker than up on the surface. Amy was glad it was still mid-afternoon, so they had some hours before darkness and the cold that came with it, to stabilise Hoani.

Amy looked around her. There was nothing she could do about the obvious danger here and also the very damp conditions. They both went over to the crumpled body that lay before them. Amy could see immediately that Hoani had an open fracture to his leg, and she wasn't happy with the position of his spine either.

"Have you a spinal board in there? Amy asked Dave as she leaned forward to check Hoani's response.

"Hoani, its Amy here. Can you hear me?" She put her hand in his. "Squeeze my hand if you can hear me." There was no response. She squeezed his shoulder and his thumb nail, but still no response. Amy then checked Hoani's pulse and breathing.

"We have a pulse and he is breathing, though it is shallow."

"That's a good start." Dave replied as he opened the pack and brought out the board.

"He's unconscious. I don't suppose you have an airway in there?"

Dave handed a bag with a variety of airways to Amy. She choose one that was his size and swiftly put it in place.

"Do we have anything to put over the board to wrap Hoani in, to keep him warm?"

Dave pulled out some foil. The board and foil were placed beside Hoani, with the foil tucked as far as they could under Hoani without moving him.

"We need to treat him as though he has both head and spinal injuries, along with that broken leg. Have we something to tie his legs together?"

Dave pulled out a couple of wide bandages, but the present position of Hoani's body made it difficult to bring them together, so it was decided to do it after Hoani was on the board.

"Do you have experience in spinal holds?" Amy asked Dave.

He shook his head.

"I will take his head and shoulders. I need you to bring his body over, keeping it in line with his head. We will do it very slowly."

Inch by inch they moved Hoani untill Amy was satisfied Hoani was in the right position on the board. The satellite phone had been ringing, but they had ignored it till now.

At the top of the Crevasse, Hori had been listening intently for the conversation down below. He heard enough to know that Hoani was being treated. He wept tears of relief that his son was still alive. He didn't care about what the future held. They would deal with that later. Down at the Heliport the family was waiting anxiously at reception for news. The receptionist had been calling Dave's satellite phone, with no answer.

"It can only mean good news." She told them. "The fact they aren't answering, means that your son is alive and they are too busy helping him to get back to us."

When Dave eventually answered the phone, she was told that they needed the team to rescue and transfer to Christchurch. She was also asked to hand the phone to the doctor in the team, who were waiting expectantly for news of whether this was to be a rescue or recovery mission.

"You've done well" was the doctor's only comment, before he sent the team out the door to the waiting helicopters. He quickly spoke to Kohi to tell her of Hoani's injuries, before he joined them.

When Terry heard the extent of Hoani's injuries, he knew it would be some time before he would hear from Amy. Myrtle was comforting Kohi, who was shedding tears of relief, but also worried about Hoani's condition. He turned to Frank who had been sitting beside him and chatting about the plants he had intended to grow. Terry also had accepted Frank's offer of help in the nursery.

"Shall we head back to Hokitika? We can't do anything more here now. I expect it will take some time to get Hoani out of that Crevasse, then time to get him over to Christchurch and start treatment. It will be tomorrow before we will know how he's going."

"You're right. It's best to get back now as we have an early start to take Kohi, Reka and Lucy over to Christchurch. Will you be coming over?"

"Normally I would, but the builder has started the renovation on my house and wants me around for any issues that needs my input. I also promised Amy I would look after Lizzie."

It was late afternoon when the sound of multiple helicopters coming up the valley alerted Hori that more help was coming. It was getting cooler up here too! He was glad he had thought to put a jacket on!

62

Down in the crevasse, Amy and Dave also could hear the helicopters and were glad that more help was coming. Hoani was starting a rouse a little, and was moaning with pain. Amy knew the leg fracture would have to be reduced soon, as the pulses in his foot were poor and hard to detect. They would need pain relief that the doctor was bringing with him, before they could treat his leg.

Hori was also glad to see the arrival of the team, who scurried across the snow to him, with various packs and a cradle stretcher for Hoani to be carried in. Hori was also given a suit to put on. He needed to be protected from the cold too, given that they didn't know how long it would take to get Hoani out of the crevasse.

Two of the team stayed up the top while the doctor lead the rest of the team down to join Dave and Amy. Hori watched as they attached ropes to the stretcher, ready to lower it down to the team below. Hori also noticed that a larger helicopter had come to land on the ice. He knew that this was their transport. He noticed that they were putting portable lights on down in the crevasse.

The doctor came over with a small pack that he handed to Amy. A blood pressure cuff, temperature scanner and an oxygen saturation monitor, which she quickly placed on Hoani's ear lobe – it was warmer than his fingers, for a more accurate reading. As the machine made its steady beeps, Amy also did Hoani's temperature and blood pressure, noting the readings in the small pad that came in the pack. While Amy was taking Hoani's observations, the doctor was placing an intravenous canula in Hoani's arm.

"Temperature 35.5. Pulse 58, respirations 14, BP 95 on 62, Oxygen sats. 92% Amy advised the doctor.

"They aren't bad, considering where he is and his condition." The doctor commented. "Start him on 10 litres of oxygen." One of the team brought over a bottle of oxygen with tubing and a mask which Amy attached to Hoani. She was happy to see the reading on the oxygen monitor start to move up immediately.

Hoani gave a moan when the doctor inserted the canula into his arm.

"Has he spoken to you yet.?" The doctor asked.

"No." Amy replied. "He only started to rouse as you were coming up the valley."

"We don't want him to be awake yet." The Doctor commented as he administered some pain relief, with a small amount of sedation. He asked Dave to hold Hoani's leg above the knee while he went down to examine Hoani's fracture.

"Any pulses? The doctor asked Amy.

"Yes, but they are difficult to find."

The doctor grabbed Hoani's ankle, supporting his calf as he did so and gave a pull. The bone sliding back into place when he released Hoani's ankle. After cleaning and placing a dressing over Hoani's leg wound, he rechecked his pulses. "That's better." The doctor commented as he marked a cross on Hoani's leg with a marker pen; before going on the check Hoani's chest, abdomen, other leg and arms.

"It looks like he has done his wrist as well." The doctor commented, noting the swelling already there, and gave it a cross as well. The doctor's expression changed to a frown as he checked Hoani's pupils with a torch.

"You're right about the head injury." The doctor commented to Amy. "The quicker we get him out of here, the better!"

"Send the stretcher down!" The doctor called to the team at the top. Sandbags were placed next to Hoani's head to stop movement and a cervical collar was placed very carefully round his neck. Once the stretcher was placed next to Hoani, - they had to work around the ropes the team up the top were holding. A nylon slide sheet along with the help of the whole team made the transfer much easier and quicker than the last one.

"You head up top now, thanks Amy. We need you to be up there when Hoani is lifted out to continue his care. I will get you to start a drip and insert a catheter. Just ask for the packs, and add head circumference measurements to your 15 minute obs. The chopper will need to refuel before you take him to Christchurch."

"Thank you everyone." Amy gave the team a smile as she made her way to the rope ladder and started her climb back up.

Blankets were added before Hoani was strapped in securely. By now the light was beginning to fade on the glacier as the sun was low in the western sky. Once Amy was back up the top with Hori, they were sent over to wait by the helicopters. One of the team members up top signalled to the pilot, who started the engine on the helicopter. After a few minutes he rose into the air and came over to hover over the crevasse, a line was lowered from the cabin into the crevasse. the team crouched low so they were out of range of the rotor blades.

Once the line was attached to the stretcher, Dave gave the signal for the stretcher to be lifted. When the team up top saw Dave's signal, they  co-ordinated the pulling of the lines they were holding, to make sure the stretcher didn't swing or spin as it was pulled out of the crevasse.

Once the stretcher was laid down on the flat area near to the other helicopters. A member of the team disconnected the line so the helicopter could leave for fuel.

Amy did another set of observations, with Hori kneeling next to her, his sad eyes noting the change in his son, who was normally relaxed when sleeping, now in an unnatural state with his eyes shut and unable to communicate. He also watched Amy as she opened a pack and proceeded to set up a drip and attached it to Hoani's arm. Before Amy started Hoani's catheter procedure, she stopped to talk to Hori.

"Hoani is unconscious, so the Doctor has asked me to put in a catheter."

"Can't you wait till he wakes up and let him go normally?"

"No. It may be days before he wakes up properly. Hoani will be given plenty of fluids, which will overstretch his bladder. That will cause pain and make it harder for him to go properly when he wakes up. It's a normal thing that needs to be done in this situation."

Hori nodded, agreeing with the wisdom of Amy's words as she undid the harness to pull aside the blankets to access Hoani.

"Is there anything I can do?" Hori asked, feeling helpless.

"Yes," Amy smiled at Hori. "You can go round the other side and when I'm ready, hold the blankets out of the way."

Hori watched with interest as Amy set up the pack and cleaned her hands before putting on gloves. He winched on Hoani's behalf when the catheter was inserted, but there was no reaction from Hoani.

Hori then felt relief that Hoani was being cared for so well in a place so far from any hospital. Amy was taping the catheter tubing to Hoani's leg when the sound of the helicopter's return could be heard, coming up the valley.

"That's good timing." Amy commented as she rearranged the blankets and rolled up the pack for the team to take back to the township.

"Let us know through the Heliport how he goes." Dave commented before he and the team prepared to lift Hoani's stretcher into the helicopter.

"I will, and thank you for everything."

Keeping their heads down, Amy and Hori followed Hoani into the helicopter, where a paramedic was also waiting to help Amy care for Hoani. Everyone including Hoani were given earplugs for the journey.

"He's due for another set of obs." Amy told the paramedic, showing the page from the pad she had been using. She attached the IV fluids to a nearby hook and showed the paramedic the contents of the catheter bag, which already was a quarter full. Then from head to toe, Amy advised the paramedic of all the known and suspected injures that Hoani had. The paramedic nodded before speaking to the pilot through his microphone. Amy noticed the helicopter increase speed after his chat.

"We will be landing at the Hospital." The medic advised Amy. You have a rest for a few minutes while I do this round of obs."

"We can only wait and hope now." Amy gave Hori's hand a squeeze as Hoani was flown to an uncertain future.

# HOANI'S RECOVERY

Hori would forever remember the helicopter ride to Christchurch. During which, both Amy and the medic worked to stabilise Hoani when his blood pressure dropped and for several minutes had to breath for him with the air viva bag.

At the hospital Hori and Amy had a long wait while Hoani was assessed, scanned, then sent to theatre to repair some of his injuries, before being sent to the Intensive care Unit. They allowed Hori a quick visit once Hoani was in ICU. Hoani was still sedated when Hori saw him, but was comforted with the knowledge that Hoani was now stable and was getting the best care that they could give him.

Hori happened to look out a window. Daylight wasn't far away. He suddenly felt exhausted and needed some sleep.

"Is there anywhere around here we can put our heads down for a while?" Hori asked the Nurse Manager.

"We have a hostel for relatives to stay." The Manager informed him. "I will just get you a voucher."

Both Hori and Amy were grateful for the facilities and care they received. Given adjoining rooms, they were also given some lounge wear to change into and shown where the lounge and dining café were. The receptionist gave them their room keys, saying. We will ring your room if you are needed on the ward."

It was only after her shower, that Amy realised that she hadn't contacted Terry yet. She reached for her phone.

In Frank's van, the drive home was subdued. Myrtle sat with her arm around Kohi. Reka and Lucy huddled in the back with Kelly and Micky. Everyone was silent with their own thoughts, wondering how Hoani was.

When Frank dropped Kelly and Micky off at their home, their parents Harry and Jean came out, concerned at their lateness at returning. Terry came out with Kelly and Micky, explaining what had happened. Harry and Jean had seen Hori driving the family in the morning, noticed the family in Frank's car.

"I take it, Hori's car is still at Franz?" Terry nodded. "We will bring it back for him."

Kohi rummaged in her bag to hand the keys over. "Thank you." It was one problem less to worry about.

Claire and Lizzie came out when Frank dropped Terry off at her house. Lizzie bounded into the van to greet Lucy and Reka. Before they left, Terry gave Lucy a hug.

"Hoani will be okay, but it will take a while for him to recover."

"Do you think so?"

"I do. We have to be strong for him untill he gets his strength back."

Lucy wasn't the only one to think of Terry's words. In the coming months, Kohi and Reka drew comfort from them too.

As Hori and Amy were preparing for bed, Frank and Myrtle were preparing to take Kohi, Reka and Lucy over to Christchurch. Kohi was grateful she had some of her family there to stay with. During the coming months she made daily visits to the hospital, before Hoani was well enough to be transferred to Greymouth Hospital for rehabilitation.

Hori was only able to stay a couple of days before having to return to his job. While Hori Kohi and Reka were allowed in immediately to see Hoani, it was another twenty four hours before Frank and Myrtle, then Amy and Lucy were allowed in to see him.

Hoani was still sedated at Lucy's first visit. She was shocked at how fragile and drawn Hoani looked, while he was hooked up to machines that were monitoring him and also giving him fluids while he was still unable to respond.

"I will help you get through this!" Lucy vowed quietly as she squeezed his hand.

While Amy and Lucy were away, Lizzie became Terry's shadow. She slept next to his bed, and came to expect a walk along the tram in the mornings. The first one was extra-long – into town to visit Terry's house, where the workmen had finished restumping the new area out the back and were putting the frame work in for the floors and walls. Lizzie was happy to have a ride home in Terry's car, after he had a talk to Rick about plans he wanted for the green houses at the Kaniere Road house. After Rick had finished at Terry's house for the day, he came out with his laser measure and notebook to take measurements.

When Frank and Myrtle brought the two families home, Amy had invited them all in for dinner. Everyone except Amy was surprised to be greeted with the welcoming smell of a roast dinner, which had been prepared by Terry under Claire's instruction. This set a routine where Reka came to spend the day with Lucy while Hori was at work. He would then join the family for dinner each evening. On Friday evenings, Hori and Reka would make the trip over to Christchurch to join Kohi on her visits to the hospital during the weekend.

Hori was surprised (and relieved) one Sunday evening to come home to find that Frank had been in to mow the lawns. Terry had weeded the front garden and made a start at the back, while Amy and Lucy had been in to give the inside a good clean for him.

Although Kohi had called to tell Hori that Hoani was awake, he was relieved on his weekend visit to see that Hoani was alert and happy to see him and Reka. Hoani's head had been shaved and was sporting a row of sutures from his cranial surgery to relieve pressure from his fractured skull. He was wearing a cervical collar and spinal brace, for support untill his spinal fractures healed; along with plaster casts on his leg and wrist. Hoani tired easily and soon dozed off for a sleep. Hori noticed that Hoani was having trouble saying some of his words and some of his co-ordination was reduced. While Hoani was having a sleep, Kohi and Hori had a talk to the Nurse Manager, who was able to reassure them that with rehab, Hoani would eventually be back to normal, though it would be some months to achieve the many milestones that lay ahead.

Lucy took Reka and Lizzie out to check the mail box at the road. Among the mail was one with her name on it. She knew immediately, her exam results were here! She opened the envelope. To her relief she had passed, but she had insufficient marks to apply for the veterinarian course that she wanted. This meant she would be applying to be a veterinarian Nurse instead. Lucy realised this was a blessing in disguise as she would have had to move to Auckland to train as a vet. Now Lucy could train in Christchurch, where she could visit Hoani often while she was studying. She could also approach the vet for some experience while she was in training.

"How did you go?" Reka wanted to know.

"I will be applying to train as a vet nurse."

"That will be a disappointment for you!" Reka commented, knowing Lucy's ambition to be a Vet.

"No." Lucy's voice was firm. "It will be better in a way, as it will be easier for me to be a wildlife carer, which I want to specialise in."

Lucy and Reka sat in her room while she went online to apply for her course. To her disappointment, all the places for the beginning of the year were taken, but there were places in the mid-year intake. Lucy decided to put her application in. She would also need some work while she was waiting for her course. Lucy went to the phone book for the Vet's number. When she came back to Reka, her eyes were shining.

"I have an interview this afternoon!"

"What interview?" Amy's voice came from the hallway. She had heard Lucy talking on the phone while she was bringing some vegetables in from the garden.

"I have an interview with the Hoki Vet this afternoon. What should I wear?"

"Something smart casual?" Amy suggested.

"Call me when you have finished." Amy told Lucy when she dropped her off at the Vets. Amy and Reka went to Terry's house to see how the work was progressing while they waited for Lucy's call. Amy was surprised to see the window and door frames already in place, the roof timber supports also being made. A pile of external cladding was also waiting to be put in place. It was quite a while before Amy's phone rang to pick Lucy up. She came out with some forms.

"I start on Monday." Lucy had a big beam on her face.

"He had me help him with a couple of patients and I nearly had a possum to take home! He wants to know when the shed and paddock is ready for my carer duties."

Hoani's envelope was also waiting when Hori came home from work that evening. He put it aside to take over to Christchurch on the weekend. He knew that any plans Hoani had for the future, would have to be deferred or even changed. When Hori put the envelope on the bed for Hoani to open, he shook his head.

"You open it Dad." Hoani had a stony look on his face – as though he had already prepared for failure. Kohi also looked as Hori opened the letter inside. Kohi gave a gasp of astonishment that made Hoani look up.

"You have got 98%!" Kohi's voice rose with excitement. "You can choose whatever you want to do!"

"You can defer." Hori offered, seeing that Hoani didn't share their joy at his success.

Hoani gave a little shake of his head. "That was then. I can't see myself doing that again." Hoani could see by the looks on their faces, that both Hori and Kohi weren't happy that he was turning his back on University, so he added; "I will see how I feel once I get through rehab. I know that I can do some work for Terry when he gets his nursery going."

Hoani's knowledge that he wouldn't do well at university wasn't the only part of his future that he was adjusting to. The accident had completely dissolved Hoani's confidence to have a relationship with Lucy. He fully expected her to be away in Auckland to train as a vet. After five years he expected her to have met someone else.

It was only when Hoani transferred to Greymouth, for rehabilitation, that his view was changed. the first person to bounce into his room was Lucy. She came over to give him a big hug.

"I'm sorry I couldn't get to visit you in Christchurch!" Lucy's tone was apologetic. "but the vet has been keeping me really busy!"

Hoani couldn't help showing his astonishment. "How come you aren't at uni at Auckland?"

Lucy grinned at Hoani. "My marks weren't good enough, so I'm going to do the vet nursing course in Canterbury. There isn't a place till mid-year. The vet wants me to do it by correspondence, doing all the practice with him. And, I will soon have the shed ready to look after the animals as I wanted to do!"

The joy in her face told Hoani that Lucy wasn't at all unhappy at how her life had turned out. The thoughtful look on Hoani's face, made Lucy ask how he did with his marks.

"I'm not sure what I'm going to do." Hoani sighed. "I got really good marks in my exams – 98%. He nodded at Lucy's gasp. "But!" Hoani stopped to look Lucy in the eye. "I can't see me going to uni now. I know the accident has changed me. I won't be able to do it! Do you understand that?" Hoani's eyes were pleading for her understanding.

Lucy had tears in her eyes as she nodded her head. But then she had resolve in her tone as she grasped his good hand. "You will find something that will suit you, I know it! We just have to get you better first. It will be much easier for me to visit you now."

Hoani gave Lucy's hand a squeeze and kept hold of it.

"Thank you for being understanding. Mum and Dad didn't take it very well when I said I wasn't going to uni. I had to put them off by saying that I will see how I am when I have recovered."

"I can understand that." Lucy spoke with sympathy. "They have high hopes for your future. It is going to take time for them to adjust to the fact that your future is on a different path to the one that they expect."

"When I'm better, I will see Terry about some work in his nursery."

"You still like animals too?" Lucy asked.

"Yes, why?"

"You can help me with my animals too. They will be right next to the nursery."

Hoani grinned at Lucy. "It looks like our future is sorted." As Hoani drew her to him, all the self-doubts he had felt over the previous months melted away as they exchanged their first kiss, sealing their relationship for the future.

The sound of footsteps had them quickly separate, for Lucy to sit demurely back in the visitors chair. The nurse wasn't fooled though. The sparkle now present in Hoani's eyes and the smile he couldn't hide showed her that Lucy's visit had done Hoani more good than any therapy would ever do.

When Hori and Kohi came to visit, they couldn't believe the change in Hoani's attitude. In Christchurch he had been mopping and obviously depressed. Now, the old Hoani was returning. They had a chat with the Nurse who was caring for him before they left, asking how he had been.

"We were a bit worried about his mental state, but he had a visit from Lucy earlier, and he has been much brighter since." She added with a smile.

# THE PROPOSAL

Amy looked at the office clock. There was another two hours before her shift was due to finish. Why was time going so slowly? As Amy worked on the staff roster, a task she used to enjoy, she realised that since she took leave to get over her bereavement, that she had changed. This job no longer gave her the enjoyment and challenges it did previously. Amy was happy to know that there were several members of staff on the ward that were both capable and willing to take over her role when she was ready to relinquish it. The big question was, what was she going to do? She had another twenty five years before she was due to retire. Did she just need a change of specialty or was a completely different career beckoning her?

As Amy drove home after her shift, she thought about how a change would affect her family. Lucy would soon be living in Christchurch while she trained to be a vet nurse. They preferred students to be at the college, but she had the advantage of having her practice already organised. Lucy vowed she would be home for the weekends. Hoani was finally out of hospital. He came over to their house every day to help Lucy with the animals that she brought home from the Vets. He would also be helping Terry and Frank with the plants in the Nursery when it was finished. Hori and Kohi hadn't been happy that Hoani had turned his back on university studies, but he had convinced them that staying here to help Terry with the nursery, and helping Lucy with her animals, was where he wanted to be.

It had taken time to get the council approval for both the business and the Green House for the plants. The concrete pad and Metal framework was now up for the Green house. They were waiting for the cladding and louver windows which would give both light and ventilation for the plants. The plant stands and reticulation system were now in the shed, after Terry's furniture had been moved into his house. Work was being done on the ensuite for the front bedroom. Once that was finished they would be able to complete the spare bedroom space. Amy didn't know it, but that room would be used for a completely different purpose!

Amy did a detour to Terry's house in Revell Street, to see how things were progressing. She was surprised to find the workmen gone and the house locked. *Had they finished the ensuite already?*

When Amy turned into her drive on Kaniere Road, the answer lay in front of her. All the workmen's cars were on her property. Rick and Terry were supervising them in installing the cladding and Louvers. The plumber was also there installing the bathroom and sinks for the staff area and connecting the reticulation up to the water supply. The electrician was also there, connecting the power to the staff area and also for the reticulation. When the workmen left, that evening, Terry's greenhouse was ready for use.

"It's finally done at last!" Terry greeted Amy as she joined him. "Will we have dinner in town tonight, to save you cooking?"

"Sounds good." Amy responded with a smile. In truth, she didn't feel like going out again, but she didn't mind having a night off making the dinner. Amy went off to have a shower and change.

She was relieved she had no further shifts this week. As Amy changed, she noticed that her clothes were tighter than usual. She made a mental note to go on a diet! She had a rummage in the wardrobe for something more comfortable.

Lucy came in as Amy was finishing changing. "We are having dinner in town tonight. Do you want to change or go as you are?"

"Thanks Mum, but I will make myself something easy. I want to do some painting." She cast a critical eye over her mother's choice of dress. "you look beautiful in that outfit. You should wear it more often."

Given that Amy was feeling anything but beautiful, she gave Lucy a big hug. "Thank you. I'm not feeling particularly beautiful, but it's nice you think so."

Lucy immediately picked up on her mother's negative feelings. "What's up Mum?"

Amy sighed. "I'm not sure. Maybe I need a change of job or specialty at work, but I'm feeling jaded and frumpy!"

Lucy laughed. "There is no way that you are frumpy! Go and enjoy your dinner!"

As Amy and Lucy left the room, Terry came in to change. Casting an appreciative eye over Amy, he too made a comment that left Amy wondering.

"I see I will have to get my best glad rags on to match!" And, true to his word, Terry also dressed with more care than usual.

At the restaurant, the waitress recognised them, and asked, "Would you like the table you had last time?"

"Yes please." Terry replied with delight. It was near the window, with a good view of the sunset. He had missed the sunsets out at the Kaniere Road house.

As they sat down and waited to order, he couldn't help referring to their last visit, for their first lunch together. "We've achieved a lot since our last visit. I think this calls for a celebration."

"What are we celebrating today? Amy asked with a smile. She didn't realise it, but she was looking radiant.

"Our house is nearly finished, and my business will soon be up and running." Terry paused to take in the beauty that sat before him. "And also to us."

"Just one glass for me." Amy specified, when the waitress came to order their meal and their drinks. Terry was going to order a bottle of wine, but followed Amy's lead and ordered a glass of beer.

"To us!"

"To us! And your business!"

"We should go for a trip to Franz again soon." Terry mentioned, while they were waiting for their dinner to arrive.

Amy's face was a picture, as astonishment showed on her face.

"I don't mean another family day like last time." Terry hastened to add, with a grin. "I was just thinking of the two of us going, with a session at the Hot pools and some lunch."

"No climbing on the glacier?" Amy couldn't help a grin as she asked.

"Definitely no climbing on the glacier!" Terry agreed. "Maybe a gentle stroll by some of those lakes that we zipped past."

When their dinner arrived. Terry brought up Lucy's move to Christchurch. "Lucy will be moving to Christchurch soon. Will she be wanting us to take her over?" Terry asked.

"She will be taking herself over. Lucy has been having driving lessons and will sit her licence shortly. She intends to buy a car." Amy grinned at Terry's astonishment. "You have been too busy with the house and organising the business to notice. She wants to come home on the weekends. It would be much easier if she drove herself instead of waiting for us to go over for her and take her back after the weekend."

Terry realised the common sense in this plan, but was disappointed he wouldn't get a trip over the pass any time soon. Amy sensed Terry's disappointment and gave him some hope.

"We can always go for a trip over the pass to visit Lucy, to see how she is settling in."

"That's a good idea."

Before they went home, Amy went to the Ladies to freshen up. In there, she met Maureen from the Travel agency, who floored Amy by commenting.

"You are looking obsolutely blooming! When is it due?" At Amy's astonished look, Maureen continued in a reproving tone. "Amy! Don't tell me you haven't noticed! You being a Nurse too!" With that Maureen swept out the door.

After Maureen left, Amy took the time to take a good look in the mirror. She realised that Maureen was right. She hadn't looked like this since she had Michael and Lucy. It also explained her weight gain, and her loss of enthusiasm for her job. Thinking back, she now knew how it happened. When she took Hoani over to Christchurch, she didn't take her medication. It also meant that this little one would be here in four to five months! Amy now wondered how Terry – and Lucy would take the news. Terry noticed that Amy had a pensive look on her face when she rejoined him.

80

"Is everything alright?" Terry asked.

"Its fine." Amy replied. "Can we go for a ride down to the strip before we go home?"

At the parking area, Terry turned the motor off as they watched the waves roll in over the bar, to clash with the water flowing from the river to the sea.

Amy turned to Terry with anxious eyes. "You won't be ready for this, and I aren't either. I'm pregnant."

"Are you sure?"

Amy nodded. All the signs are there and other people are noticing!" Amy added with a wry smile. "I'm pretty sure it happened after I took Hoani to Christchurch. I will get a test from the chemist tomorrow to confirm it."

"Who's noticing it?" Terry was interested to know.

"Maureen from the travel Agency was asking me when it was due! So the whole town will know shortly!"

Terry leant over to take Amy in his arms. "It's a shock, but I'm thrilled! I gave up the idea of having a family long ago. Now, here it is, whether we are ready or not!" Terry gave a chuckle. "You do realise we will have to get hitched again!"

Amy pulled herself away. "We don't have to do anything!"

Terry pulled her back again. "I know we don't, but I want to!" The tone in Terry's voice made Amy look at him.

"Will you marry me?"

The humility in Terry's voice left Amy in no doubt that the old Terry was well and truly gone. That she was safe with the man that wanted her to take his name again.

"Yes, though there is no rush. We wouldn't be the first family to have the baby at the wedding."

"How long have we got?

"About four to five months."

"It would be nice though to have our honeymoon or should we call it Babymoon before it comes."

Amy collapsed into a fit of giggles.

"Alright, you win! Where do you want the ceremony? In town or at the Bach?"

"If its fine, we will have it at the bach. If its slashing with rain, we can have it in town. Speaking of which; it is just as well that I had the upstairs room added to the Revell street house. The second bedroom can be the baby's room. We will sleep in the front room for now, but I may look at putting in an upstairs room for us There is enough room up there for a bedroom as well as the office and craft area."

"We will have to make changes to the Kaniere Road House too. Lucy will have to make room in the shed for her painting things."

Amy gave a little sigh.

"What's up?"

"I'm not sure how Lucy will react to having a much younger sister or brother."

Amy need not have worried, though. When they returned home, Lucy and Claire were waiting for them. Both of them were looking at Amy's waistline and were grinning. Lucy came over to give her mother a big cuddle.

"I'm looking forward to having another brother or sister."

Amy looked at Terry with alarm. "I didn't expect the grapevine to spread that fast!"

Claire laughed, before adding "I had a phone call from Maureen!   I've got my orders to make sure you look after yourself!  I expect you will be going on leave soon?"

"I will do, though I will be organising a replacement for my job."

"You won't be going back afterwards?"

"Not this time.  I'm not sure what I will do yet, but I feel it is time for a new career." Amy patted her stomach. "Whatever I do, this little one (and the family) will come first."

Terry put his arm around Amy. "She won't have time for working anyway, as we have a wedding to organise."

There were gasps of delight from both Claire and Lucy.  The remainder of the evening was spent in planning for the wedding.

For Amy, the next week, were spent in a whirl of tests and checks.  At the ultra sound, the technician took extra time to check the baby.

"Is anything wrong?"  Amy was alert for anything out of the ordinary, though she couldn't see anything wrong.

The technician gave her a smile.  It is hard to see, but I think you may be having twins.  Is there a history of twins in your family?  The second one is hiding well behind the front one.  Can you see the extra arm here and there?"

"So that's why I've been getting back ache!"

Amy was given confirmation that her babies were due in four months.  She also had to organise a handover for her replacement.  She was relieved when one of her senior nurses was given her position.

The day Amy packed up her desk for the last time was both bitter and sweet. The end of her job here after eighteen years was a wrench, but Amy was more than ready now for a break.

Amy had a sort through her wardrobe, putting in storage clothes she wouldn't need again untill well after the baby was born. As she was sorting, Amy came across a dress that she had forgotten about, A floaty pink chiffon. On impulse, she tried it on. It still fitted perfectly, though the shoes that went with it didn't. Amy turned to the sound of noise behind her. Lucy gave a gasp of amazement!

"I see you have your wedding dress sorted! Will you be wearing those shoes?"

Amy shook her head. Lucy immediately grabbed them and shot off to her room. Several minutes later, Lucy returned in a baby pink draped crepe dress, which accented all of her curves. The shoes fitted her perfectly. She stood next to her mother to look in the mirror.

"I think we are ready, except for some flowers!"

# THE FIRE

During this time, Terry was also busy. Both Frank and Hoani were helping him set up the stands for the plants and also setting up the potting area. They already had a supply of seeds, thanks to numerous walks in the forest, and also had harvested seeds from local native trees and shrubs that they had noticed were carrying seeds. Terry brought out a thick book on New Zealand plants for them to make labels of the seeds they were planting.

They were having a break when Hoani asked Terry a question.

Will you be having a section for medicinal plants?

Terry looked at him with astonishment, but smiled.

"It sounds like a good selection for us to have. Do you have a book on them at home by any chance?"

It was Hoani's turn to be perplexed. "I don't think so, but Aunty Moana at the pa knows a lot about them."

"If you have a look at home for any books, I will look on the internet. If neither of us find the information we need, then you need to contact your Aunty Moana and ask her if she can tell you everything she knows. Tell her that we don't want her knowledge to be lost."

A couple of days later, when Hoani came in, he had Moana with him. Terry could see immediately that she was Hori's sister.

"Hello Moana." Terry greeted her. She gave him a smile, but Moana had wide eyes as she looked at the big bright covered space. Much of the floor space was taken with rows of tables. Many tables now had punnets of seeds on them.

"What did you want to know?" Moana asked, after taking in the space before her.

"Hoani is interested in growing medicinal plants. He mentioned that you have a lot of knowledge about them. We want to know the names of the plants. What they look like. Where they grow. What flowers and fruit or seeds they have, and most importantly what medicinal uses they have and how they are prepared."

Moana looked alarmed. "I'm not sure I know all that!"

"Perhaps you can take Hoani out to places where you know plants are and show him the plants you know, and tell him what you know about them."

"Will you remember what I tell you?" Moana was doubtful.

Hoani grinned. "I will bring a camera and a note pad with me. I will take photos of the plants and write down the details that you tell me. I'm thinking that I will make it into a book that we can sell with the plants. Would you like it to be called "Moana's Medicines?" Perhaps some of the proceeds can go to a cause or charity that you like to support?"

Moana thought about what Hoani said. She gave him a smile.

"You're a good boy for your Whanau." Moana then turned to face Hoani. Her face was solemn. "The knowledge comes with responsibilities. Are you prepared to become a healer?"

"I am." Hoani replied, equally seriously.

"You may not have time for this when you become a healer." Moana warned Hoani.

"No!" Hoani's voice was firm. "This job is equally important and complimentary to healing.

86

Without the nurturing of plants and making sure they are available to future generations; healing will die out. We can't just rely on the forest to provide us with plants. If anything happens we can lose them completely."

Moana nodded at the wisdom of Hoani's words. She looked around. "What plants have you got here?"

Hoani gave her a tour of the greenhouse. As they were going around, Moana started making comments about the plant they were looking at.

"Just a second." Hoani stopped her, and shot over to the office where he collected a pad and pen out of his bag. By the time they finished the tour, Hoani had several pages of notes.

"I will walk you back to our house." Hoani told Moana. We will go out for a walk this afternoon."

"I can give you a lift." Terry offered them. "I am heading into town to check on the house shortly."

"Thank you." Moana accepted Terry's offer of a lift. Afterwards, the family would be forever grateful that Terry was there.

Terry stopped in the driveway to let Moana and Hoani out. Once they were out of the car, Terry was about to put the car in reverse, when the sight of smoke coming from the back of the house stopped him. Then to his horror he saw flames! Terry swiftly turned off the motor. And got out of the car as Hoani and Moana approached the front door.

"STOP! DON"T OPEN THE DOOR!" Terry yelled at Hoani.

As they turned to see what Terry was yelling for, the sound of breaking glass and the roar of flames could be heard at the back of the house. Terry motioned for them to come to him, as he got his phone out and called emergency services for the Fire Brigade.

"Where is your mother and Reka?" Terry wanted to know when he had got off the phone.

Panic immediately came over Hoani's face. "Mum was in the kitchen out the back and Reka was still in bed when I left."

"What room is Reka sleeping in?"

"The first one on the right."

"Stay out here and look after Moana!" Terry instructed him.

Gingerly Terry felt the front door knob. It didn't feel hot, which was a good start. Hoani came to unlock the door. As Terry inched the door open, thick smoke poured out. Hoani immediately moved away to comfort Moana, who was in tears. Terry knelt down on his hands and knees to look down the hallway, which was filled with smoke. He thought he could see a foot. Bringing his shirt up over his nose and mouth, Terry crawled down the hallway and tried not to breath in the smoke, feeling the floor as he went. To his relief, it was a foot he had seen, and immediately pulled it towards him. Steadily he pulled the body down the hallway. He didn't hear the fire engines arrival. He was nearly at the door when a firm hand on his shoulder and a voice saying "We will take over now." before Terry knew that help was here.

"There's another one in there." Terry managed to say and pointed to the bedroom. The fireman immediately stepped over them to head for the bedroom. Luckily the door had been shut, so Reka hadn't been disturbed by the smoke, but she was alarmed to wake to her door being opened and a fireman in full breathing apparatus come in, with smoke wafting in around him, before he shut the door.

"Your house is on fire. We have to get you out. Does your window open?"

Reka managed to nod her head. The fireman swiftly opened the curtains and blind to open the window, before yelling out for a ladder. Reka could hear the sound of the water pump and other members of the team calling to each other as they worked to put out the blaze.

As Terry pulled Kohi out through the front doorway, willing hands came to carry Kohi away from the house and administer oxygen to her. Someone else came to help Terry walk away from the house. He too was given some oxygen, which immediately made him feel better.

An ambulance came to attend to Kohi. By the time they were ready to leave for Greymouth Hospital, she was beginning to return to consciousness, much to everyone's relief. They wanted to take Terry too, but he refused.

"I'm feeling much better now. I will take it easy today." Terry promised.

"If you have any problems at all with your breathing or tightness in your chest, you are to call an ambulance!" The ambulance office ordered him in a reproving tone.

"I will." Terry promised.

Word had got to the Depot where Hori worked. His car came speeding down the road, in time for him to be with Kohi as they took her through to Greymouth. Terry noticed his car had been moved from the driveway. Hoani and Moana were sitting in it, watching everything that was going on. Reka joined them once she had been helped out of her room.

Terry's phone rang.  It was Rick.  "Are you coming in today?"

"I was, but a fire got in the way.  What's up?"

"Not at Amy's place?"

"No.  It's at Hori's."

"We've finished the ensuite.  I just want your final approval."

"I will ring you when I can come in.  I will have to wait till they've put the fire out and take Hori's sister and his children over to Amy's house."

The chief fire officer came to talk to Terry once the fire was out.

"The Kitchen, Laundry and Bathroom have been gutted.  They will need to live somewhere else while the house is being repaired.  It looks like an electrical fault started it."

"I will just give Amy a ring and see if they can stay at her place."

Once Terry got off the phone, he was able to give the officer good news.

"We can help them with that." Terry advised him.

"Do you kids want to get some clothes from your rooms?"  Terry asked them once he returned to the car.  It's going to be a while before you can live here again.  You are coming to live at Amy's house."

Terry and Moana went back into the house with them to help them, which was just as well, as everything that hadn't been burnt, had suffered some water damage.  The house reeked of both smoke and burnt furniture, which both Hoani and Reka were glad to get away from.  The car boot was full by the time they left.

"You can always come back if you have forgotten something." Terry advised them, as they left the house.

At Amy's, Frank and Myrtle were waiting with Amy to give Hoani and Reka a hug. Lucy happened to have the day off work at the vets, also came to take charge of Reka, who belatedly realised that she needed a shower and a change of clothes from her pyjamas! Lunch was a quiet affair, as everyone was wondering how Kohi was getting on.

After lunch, Amy took Lucy into town. It was time for Lucy to take her driving test. While she was waiting for Lucy's call, Amy had cleared her paintings and equipment from the spare room to the shed. So a bed could be made up for Hoani in there. Reka was sharing Lucy's room for the night and Hori and Kohi would have Amy and Terry's room when they returned. When Terry went into town to see Rick, his car was full of his clothes and gear.

Lucy was both relieved and excited to pass her test. With much pride, she put on her "P's" to drive home. It was only later in the afternoon, after Amy received a call from Hori at the Hospital saying that Kohi was improving, with no apparent damage from the smoke but was being observed overnight; that everyone relaxed.

Frank and Myrtle took his van, while Amy and Lucy took Hoani and Reka back to their house to pack up as many valuables as they could salvage, as she wasn't sure how safe items in the house would be, now that the house couldn't be secured. Several trips later, everything of value was now safe in Amy's shed. By now Amy was feeling tired and sore, but kept going as there was much left to do. It didn't help that little feet were pounding her stomach!

"Keep something to wear tomorrow, but pack all your clothes into the car." Amy advised Lucy.

Once Lucy removed her clothes from the wardrobe, Reka was putting her possessions in.

"You shouldn't take everything." Reka told her. "This is still your home. When you come home on the weekends, you will want something here, even if It's only a few things. We would love for you to stay with us on Friday nights then go to stay with your mum for the rest of the weekend."

Lucy saw the wisdom of this idea, and between them they selected a few outfits for Lucy to keep here, including a jacket, boots and shoes.

After dinner, Moana was taken home, with a promise to drop Hoani off the next day so she and Hoani could go for their bush search while Terry went to pick up Hori and Kohi.

While Terry was taking Moana home, Amy and Lucy took their possessions in to the Beach house. They set up the couch as a bed for Lucy the following night. She loved the wardrobe with the stained glass door for her clothes.

"Don't get too attached to that wardrobe." Amy smiled at her. "The children will be in this room and once we put on an extra bedroom upstairs; you will have the front room.

Lucy looked at her mother with astonishment. "How many children are you planning to have?"

Amy smiled. "I wasn't planning on having any, but it looks like I'm having twins!"

The next morning Terry took Hori and Kohi to the remains of their home. Hoani had been picked up after his outing with Moana, but chose not to come. In silence, they took in the damage.

Terry noticed with a frown that certain items that had been left behind were now missing.

"What's up?" Hori saw Terry's frown.

"I'm glad we moved everything of value into our shed. Someone's been in overnight to steal everything we left behind."

Afterwards Terry took them to their new home at Amy's house. Before he took them in the house, he unlocked the shed to show them what had been salvaged for them. They couldn't help noticing the smell of smoke through everything, especially the clothes.

"We will have to wash everything, and air it before we can use it." Hori turned to Terry. "We owe you our gratitude. You not only saved Kohi's and Reka's life; we didn't expect to have anything at all from the house."

On the verandah, Amy had an early lunch waiting.

"I could get used to this!" Hori said, taking in the view of the fields with the orchard and bushland beyond. He also noticed how much quieter it was here, compared to their home on Kaniere Road.

"Remember, your back at work tomorrow!" Kohi reminded him.

When Amy gave them a tour of the house and showed Kohi and Hori their room; Kohi had tears in her eyes.

"What's the matter?" Amy asked as she put her arm around her. "Is the shock of everything catching up with you?"

"No, it's not that. It's just that I've never slept in such a beautiful room before! They are tears of happiness!"

By the time Hori and Kohi went to bed that night, he also knew how Kohi felt. He too loved it here, but how would they be able to stay here? He knew that Amy would never sell it as it would one day be Lucy's. Hori smiled to himself. It was handy that Hoani was keen on Lucy and she felt the same about him. They would need someone to look after the property untill they were ready to take over the care of it. He and Kohi had plenty of time to find a way to continue living here too. With that thought, Hori had the best sleep he had had for a long time.

As Amy Terry and Lucy settled into the Beach house, there was one member of the family that wasn't happy in the new house. Lizzie was completely restless, not settling anywhere. Terry took her for a walk, but it didn't make any difference.

"She's missing the old house." Terry commented. "I will take her out with me in the morning. I will see if Hori will take care of her if she doesn't want to come back with me."

Amy was sad that Lizzie wasn't going to stay here with them, but she understood. Lizzie had spent most of her life at the Kaniere Road house, with the occasional night at Claire's.

"Come here girl." Amy called Lizzie to her. As Lizzie came to over for a pat, putting her head in Amy's lap, Amy leant over to give her a hug. It was then that Lizzie heard the heart beats inside Amy's stomach. She understood immediately that Amy was having human pups! She gave Amy's stomach a sniff before settling down next to her. From then on, She rarely let Amy out of her sight untill the babies were born.

# THE WEDDING

The week before Lucy went to Christchurch to live was a busy one. Frank and Hoani looked after the nursery while Terry took Lucy up to Greymouth to look for a car. When they returned, Lucy was driving a sedan that was capable of four wheel drive. Lucy had preferred a sporty little mini, but Terry reminded her that she would be making frequent trips over Arthurs Pass, and she needed something that would handle the conditions she might encounter in the winter months and made sure that a set of chains was in the boot. Lucy had a test run in putting them on before she left.

The highlight of the week for Lucy, was on the Saturday, which dawned clear with crisp frost on the lawn as winter days lay ahead. Hori and Kohi slept in her room at the bach while Lucy and her friends slept in the main room. For once Amy had the bed to herself – after so many months of sharing it again, it seemed strange to be alone and was glad it was only for one night. When Terry needed to share her home, Amy had already accepted that the intimate relationship she had previous shared with him would return. Terry was sleeping in town for the night. Frank and Myrtle were going to bring him out later.

As the early morning sun penetrated the curtains of the living area, Lucy slipped out of her camp bed and pattered over to the door. She smiled as she noticed Hovea Hedgehog waddle from the shed to the garden. She was followed by Wesley Weka. Lucy saw with horror, a Harrier come into a tree next to the garden and was eyeing Hovea and Wesley as they searched for their feed.

Swiftly Lucy opened the door and ran onto the verandah and clapped her hands loudly at the harrier, which immediately flew off over the lake. Hovea curled up in a ball at the noise Lucy was making, and Wesley shot back behind the shed, but after hearing the sound of large wing beats departing overhead, Hovea realised that Lucy was protecting her from a large bird! Slowly Hovea unwound and called to Wesley to continue their search of the garden, while Lucy sat on the back steps to watch them.

Hoani woke to the sound of Lucy opening the back door and came to see what she was doing, just in time to see the harrier fly off. He looked up at Mount Tahua, and the sky in the west, it was clear.

"Would you like a hike before breakfast?" Hoani asked, looking at Tahua.

"Have we got time?"

"We should be back by nine."

When they returned inside, Reka, Kelly and Micky were already dressing and packing up the beds. They knew that an adventure was being organised. Lucy left a message that they should be back by nine, before picking up her little backpack that she always took hiking.

Amy heard Lucy and her friends leave in the car, but promptly went back to sleep. She trusted them to be careful, wherever they were going. She also knew they had no intention of missing the ceremony. Lucy took the car to the start of the Mount Tahua trail where they piled out and began the trek up the mountain, which was a gentle incline at first, but became more challenging as they clambered up the slopes. It was with both relief and delight when they reached the summit. The clear views all around them made the climb worthwhile.

"I'm going to miss you!" Hoani began. He had to restrain himself from saying "Don't fall in love with anyone over there!"

Lucy laughed. "You would think I was going away for months or years! – I will be back next weekend!"

"We will still miss you!" Kelly added. "Are you still looking after the animals Hoani, while Lucy is away? We would like to come and help, if you are."

"In that case, I will get you to come with me to see the vet when he gives me the next animal that he wants me to care for."

On their way back down again, they had to take extra care in case they slipped. No-one wanted to get injured now. Back at the car, they were hot and sweaty, so they stripped off to their underwear and had a dip in the lake. It was well after nine when they returned to the bach. It was only the fact that Claire had also been for a swim further down the bay and seen them enter the water, that Amy, Hori and Kohi had been reassured that all was well.

After quickly consuming their breakfast, they helped set up the back garden for the ceremony. Chairs were put out on the lawn, with a table in front. The garden was raided for flowers and ferns for both the table and for bouquets for Amy and Lucy. Wesley Weka woke Hovea from her sleep in the shed.

"Something is going on in Amy's backyard!"

Hovea took one look and agreed that something important was going to happen. She spotted Foxglove Fantail in the trees and told her to call everyone! Animals and birds came from near and far to get a view, including Oriel Owl the Kingdom guardian. With him was Hagar, the spirit Harrier, who was wondering why these humans were so special in all the animals' lives.

*These humans are special.* Oriel read Hagar the spirit Harriers' leaders thoughts. *Because the female Amy, is the ancestor of Emily who first brought books and left them with us. Orion Owl was the first guardian of the Kingdom. He learnt to read and write human language from Emily. When we want books ,we come to Amy.*

*When do you want more books?*

*When a new community school in the Kingdom is created.*

*How many schools have you got?*

Oriel had to think for a few minutes. *We have seven so far. That's one less than all the claws on your feet.*

Hagar looked down at all of his claws and realised how extensive the kingdom now was.

Indoors, preparations were in full swing. Claire and her girls had arrived, with the wedding cake. The table was now reset for a buffet lunch, with plates and glasses ready. Kohi and Hori were already dressed for the occasion, Hori checking the supplies of drinks while Kohi checked that the food was ready.

Hoani and Micky had been sent off to get ready first as they took less time than the girls. Once they emerged from Lucy's room, which had been designated the change room, Lucy, Reka and Kelly took their turn to change. Amy had retreated to her room with Claire to change. Once into her outfit, she faced the mirror.

"Will I do?" she asked Claire.

"You are perfect!" Claire declared to the radiant figure beside her.

Outside, the sound of car doors could be heard.

"They are here." Claire spoke. I will go and let them in."

She went to the front door, but Hori and Kohi had heard the car come too and already had the door open to welcome Frank and Myrtle. Terry and the Vicar were also with them.

"I see you made sure he didn't get let behind!" Hori joked to Frank and the Vicar.

"We could always have used you as his proxy!" The vicar joked back.

"We are all ready." Claire said to the vicar and to Terry.

Myrtle quickly popped in to see Amy as Hori and Kohi lead the vicar and Terry outside. Claire sent the young ones outside and brought Lucy in to her mother. Myrtle gasped and had tears in her eyes when she saw the stunning beauty that Lucy had become.

Amy nodded when she saw Myrtle's emotion.

"Her father would be very proud. I'm sure he's with us in spirit."

Myrtle and Claire gave Amy and Lucy a hug before she and Claire led them out to the backyard. As Amy reached the back steps she stopped. She was aware that all of her animal family were here too! She took the time to look around at all the trees and the back garden to give them a smile.

"What's she looking at?" Hori wanted to know.

Hoani had to take his eyes off Lucy to see what Hori was talking about.

"Amy is welcoming her animal family." Hoani told him. "They have come to see her too."

Hori hadn't noticed the animals before, but when he looked around at both the trees and garden, it was full of birds and animals, looking at Amy.

Terry took a deep breath when he saw Amy approaching. He had taken her for granted last time. It had taken eighteen long years for him to appreciate the vision that was returning to his life. He meant to make the most of the second opportunity that fate had given him. Terry smiled as Amy stopped to see her animal family. He had spotted them when he came out too!

When the time came for their vows to love and to cherish, Terry looked into Amy's eyes with a look that told her that he meant every word.

Much later, when Hori and Kohi were about to take their leave, Hoani spoke to Lucy.

"You are leaving tomorrow. Come and see us before you leave."

"I will."

When Lucy pulled up in the driveway, Kohi and Reka were waiting to take her inside where Hori and Hoani were waiting.

"Lucy," Hori began. "To us, you are already Whanau. To keep you close, while you are away from your Whanau, we have a Taonga for you to wear." Hori gave Hoani a Pounamu pendant carved in the shape of a Koru, which was hung on a woven leather cord. Hoani came forward to put it over her head before he pressed his nose and forehead to hers.

"Nga Mihi, toku Aroha." (Thank you, my love.) Lucy responded before also looking at Hori Kohi and Reka. "Nga Mihi, toku Whanau" (Thank you my Family).

After Lucy left for her new life in Christchurch, Amy and Terry packed Lizzie and their bags into his car. They too were heading away.

They were heading south again for the break that Terry had promised himself – a leisurely look at all the lakes on the way to Franz Joseph Glacier. Lizzie enjoyed all the stops on the way to explore new places and smells!

When Terry and Amy took themselves off to the Thermal pools, for a welcome soak in a private pool, Lizzie was happy to stay and be fussed over by the receptionist.

# HORI AND KOHI'S NEW HOME

As Hori drove past his old home on his way to work, he knew had a big decision to make. What was he going to do with it? He knew that neither Kohi nor the children wanted to return there to live again, even if it was repaired back to the way it had been before the fire. Should he repair it and sell it or just demolish it for someone else to start with a readymade section? One thing he did want to do, was to take some seeds and cuttings from the trees and plant them on Amy's section. He would do that on the way home.

After Reka had departed for school on her bike and Hoani had seen to the animals – he had a possum, a Tui and a Weka in the shed. Secure aviaries had been attached so the animals could go outside for a run or fly if they chose. Hoani was now busy checking the plants in the glasshouse before he spent time on his computer, compiling the book that he had promised for Moana. Kohi did a quick tidy of the house before Millie the cleaner arrived. Amy had employed Millie while she was working and Kohi was quick to accept her offer to stay on after Amy had moved into the town. Millie was also cleaning Amy's new home as well.

After greeting Millie, Kohi took herself out to her favourite place – Her easel in the shed. She left the door open for the light she needed, and once again wished there were some more windows in here! She had to shut it again as the light dimmed and a shower of rain came through. While she was waiting for the rain to stop, Kohi looked around at the big space in the shed where the animals and all the equipment and food for them was on one side.

The remainder of the ground floor was open. Some of their furniture and belongings still remained for them to clean, but plenty of room remained for both Kohi and Lucy's painting equipment, as well as an area for Hoani to set up his healing centre when he was ready. Above it all was a large mezzanine area, which gave Kohi an idea. Carefully, she climbed the ladder and had a good look around at the space. It was a little dusty, which was to be expected, but the roof was water tight, and there was plenty of head height to move around.

Kohi started to imagine rooms in the space. Yes, there was room for a nice big bedroom with an ensuite. Yes, there was room for a large living area, and it would be easy to make windows to see both the Alps and the Sunset. With a little smile, Kohi descended the ladder. She would talk to Hori about it when he came home. They would also have to approach Amy and Lucy about her idea when they returned.

When Hori stopped by his old home on Kaniere Road, he noticed how unkept it was looking, and got out the lawn mower to give the lawns a much needed trim. The noise brought out his neighbour Don, for a chat.

"Hello Hori! Are you coming back then?"

Hori sighed as he came over to the fence.

"I'm not sure what to do." Hori confessed. "Kohi and the kids don't want to come back, so I have to choose whether to repair and sell it or to pull it down and let someone else build something they would like."

"What sort of price do you want for it?" Don asked. "My son is looking for a section."

Hori's eyes twinkled. "His wife doesn't mind being so close to the in-laws?"

Don laughed at Hori's in-law joke. "They are looking for somewhere that is close to us!"

"Will they want the section cleared?" Hori wanted to know.

"Don't do anything rash like that!" Don implored him. "I think they would appreciate a section with an established garden to build on. Don didn't mention that he would like some of Hori's trees and plants if his son didn't want them. "Just get a price to us that you are comfortable with, and we will go from there."

"You want what's left of the house too?"

"How much is left?"

"All the bedrooms and the lounge. Come and have a look."

As Hori let Don in, the smell of smoke was still in the house, though it wasn't as overpowering as when he last came, after the fire. Don was surprised at how intact the front of the house was, though the back where the living area had been was a black ruin, partly open to the sky. This place certainly had possibilities; Don could see. If his son wasn't interested, he certainly would like to do it up.

When Hori left, he was feeling much more hopeful than when he arrived. He also had a selection of cuttings with him. – Some had also gone next door with Don. Kohi was wondering where Hori had got to, as he was much later than usual, but Hori's grin when he came in the door, told her that all was well.

When the family sat down to dinner, Hori was able to tell them that Don was interested in buying their old house, as is. He just had to give him a price.

Kohi in turn gave Hori a floor plan. Instead of painting, she had measured the mezzanine and then worked out a plan for the area.

"What's this Mum? Hoani and Reka wanted to know.

"Hopefully, Amy will agree that this will be our new home." Kohi smiled at Hori. "There is a lovely mezzanine area in the shed that would make a lovely place for us when Hoani and Lucy take over the house."

Reka looked at the plan. "Where's my room?"

"You don't mind living in the shed with us?"

Reka grabbed the plan and a pencil and drew in another bedroom and ensuite on the other side of the living area.

Amy and Terry were still enjoying their stay at Franz Joseph township when Amy received a call. It was Hori on the phone.

"Is everything okay? Do you want us to come back?" Amy asked, thinking that there was an emergency with the house.

"No, No!" Hori hastened to reassure Amy. "Everything is all good here! We have a proposition to put to you. Can you come by when you come back?"

Mystified, Amy agreed, wondering what the proposition may be. This had both Amy and Terry guessing what it could be.

"It has to be about the house." Terry proposed. "Perhaps they want to buy it?"

"I don't think so." Amy countered. "They know I would never sell it and that it is going to Lucy. Perhaps they want to get involved in your plant nursery?"

They were floored when they met with Hori and his family to find a plan of the shed, with a living area incorporated into it. After listening to Hori and Kohi's proposal, which wouldn't cost Amy anything, they were enthusiastic.

"We will have get Lucy's approval as well, of course."

When Lucy steered her car towards Arthurs Pass mid Friday afternoon, she felt both regret and excitement at returning to the Coast. She had a full week at the college, adjusting to the routine of her new classes, making friends and also settling in to her living quarters. Lucy had her own room, but shared the big bathroom down the hall. There was a big lounge, dining room and laundry that everyone shared.

Lucy would have loved to join her friends who were getting ready to go out on the town for dinner together, but knew everyone would be disappointed if she didn't come home. She realised then, that she would have to let the family know that there would be some weekends when she would be staying in Christchurch, especially when the weather was bad or when she had assignments and exams to prepare for.

As Lucy travelled the pass, she was pleased that Terry had insisted on a bigger car, which negotiated the steep and winding road with ease. Books and notes she needed to study over the weekend were in the car with her. She was also excited to be back with her families – both Hoani and his family and Amy and Terry, not to mention Lizzie. Lucy had already called Kohi when she was at Arthur's Pass to let her know the approximate time she would be arriving, which Kohi appreciated. She had dinner ready to serve when Lucy arrived. Lucy was greeted with a kiss and a cuddle from Hoani when she emerged from the car.

"We've missed you!" Hoani said as he led her towards the house. "How has it been?"

"It's been full on!" Lucy smiled at him. "I have had to bring some homework with me!  How are the animals going?"

"They are all progressing well.  You will be able to help me release the Weka in the morning.  The Tui is feeding itself now, so no more night feeds! And the Possum's wound is healing well.  I will be able to take it to the vet to get it's stitches out next week before we release it."

After traditional greetings to Hori, Kohi and Reka, they all sat down to dinner.  Lucy told them of all the things she had learnt about, in the week, her living arrangements and the friends she had made there.

"How have things been here?" Lucy wanted to know.  She turned to Hoani. "How is the plant nursery going?"

"It is going so well; we have sent our first batch of plants off to Auckland.  They are really happy with them and want everything we can supply them."

"That's great news!  How are you going with your book and your healing?

"The file for the plants keeps growing!" Hoani grinned at her. "The healing is going well.  I will be going with Moana when she has a session next week."  Hoani glanced at Hori.  "We have some news for you to think about, and we hope you approve of it too.  We have already spoke to your mum about it and she is happy with it.  We will show you when we have finished tea."

Lucy was intrigued with this news.  She happened to have finished her meal and was waiting for everyone else to finish too.  Instead of going to clear the dishes, the family sat down in the lounge where Hoani brought out a building plan.

"Is this for the house?" Lucy asked.  She realised straight away that another level was being added.

"No, it's for the shed."  Hoani replied.  "None of us want to return to the house on the road, and our neighbour wants to buy it from us.  We are thinking of building another level where the Mezzanine is for Mum Dad and Reka when we are ready to take over the house.  The sale of the house will pay for the work on the shed."  We could call it a "Barn Conversion".  What do you think?"

Lucy looked at the plan, and liked what she saw so much that she wanted to live in it!  There was several minutes while Lucy worked it out in her mind.  The family could see by the expression on Lucy's face that she liked what she saw, but they were astonished at her proposal when she finally spoke.

"I really love it!"  Lucy's eyes were shining.  "But, I think we should be living there." Lucy turned to Hoani.  "It makes more sense for us to be upstairs than your mum and dad as time goes by.  It is better for them to stay in this house than negotiating stairs.  Given that my animals and my art are in that building and your office for your healing practice is over there, it would be much less disruptive for us to be there." Lucy had another look at the plan.  "Who was going to be sleeping on this side?  Lucy asked, pointing to the extra bedroom and ensuite that Reka had pencilled in.

"That was to be my room." Reka replied.

"I'm thinking that should be our room." Lucy proposed to Hoani.  If we sleep on this side, there will be much less disturbance for the children when I have to get up to the animals in the night.  We should put a combined bathroom and laundry on the other side of the living area, with two bedrooms for the children there.

Kohi can have the room where Hoani is now sleeping for her art. What do you all think?"

Hori had a big grin on his face. He didn't really want to move out of this lovely comfy house and Lucy had proposed the perfect solution. Kohi stole a look at him and seeing his grin knew that he had the same thought as her!

"We are happy to stay in here." Kohi spoke for them both.

"I love the room I'm in," Reka added. "I'm happy to stay in here too."

Hoani was the only one to be disappointed at not staying in the house, but when he eventually saw the views from their new home; his disappointment dissipated. He comforted himself with the knowledge that when they too grew older, they too would retreat to this house, leaving younger members of the family to stay "upstairs".

# THE NEW ARRIVALS

Amy turned over. Her back ached and she was more than ready for the arrival of the twins, though she still had a fortnight to go till their due date. Knowing she wasn't going to get any more sleep, Amy quietly slipped out of bed and padded over to the window. Red predawn light could be seen beyond the lake hills and Alps. Lizzie was immediately alert and came to sit beside her.

Terry's arms wrapped her in his embrace as she watched the morning light change from orange to gold as the sun finally peeped over the horizon.

"Can't you sleep?" Terry murmured in her ear.

"That's all I'm getting for now." Amy sighed. "I will have to have a nap later."

As Terry's hand lay lightly on Amy's stomach, he felt a distinct punch as one of the twins gave a hard kick.

"That must have hurt! I felt that!" Terry exclaimed as he gave her stomach a gentle rub.

"I sure felt that too!" Amy smiled. "It's a wonder I'm not black and blue inside!"

Later, Amy was still feeling restless, as she wandered about the house.

"Do you feel up to a trip over to Christchurch to see Lucy? It will probably be the last one before the twins come. I will get Frank and Hoani to mind the nursery."

"That's a good idea! Can you check that the motel is available?"

The motel they used was also dog friendly. When confirmation came that a room was available, they set off, with their bags and Lizzie in the back.

Lizzie was happy! The last time they had bags in the car, they went on a long adventure. As they approached Otira, Amy was finally feeling more comfortable. The twins seemed to be settling down to one of their quiet periods. They had a short stop there to give Lizzie a run around, while they admired the characters from The Lord of the Rings. Back in the car, they admired the Rata that was starting to blossom on the slopes as they crossed the pass.

At Arthur's Pass they made another stop for Lizzie, but as Amy emerged from the car, to her horror, clear liquid cascaded down her leg. - She knew that her waters had broken, followed immediately by a strong contraction! These babies weren't going to wait till they reached Christchurch!

"What's the matter?" Terry asked, seeing the horrified expression on Amy's face.

"Nothing's wrong, except that my waters have just broken and I've just gone into labour! Can you go to the shop over the road and find out where the nearest Doctor or nursing post is?"

Terry tried to hide his alarm and quickly ran across the road, while Lizzie came to sit by Amy. It was only a couple of minutes before Terry returned, with a lady from the shop. Amy was having another contraction.

"I'm Helen." She introduced herself. "How close are the contractions?"

"About two minutes apart." Amy managed to say as she tried to breathe through the contraction.

"Come with me. We aren't having it in the car park!" Helen's tone was firm, as she led Amy across the road. Lizzie was close on Amy's heels. She wasn't going to be left behind!

"Terry, can you bring my bag?" Amy called to him.

Terry didn't need to be told twice, and quickly fetched it. In the shop, Amy had to stop for another contraction, watched with interest by other shoppers in the shop, including a nurse.

"I'm Jim, and I'm a nurse. Can I help?"

"Have you done any maternity?"

"In my training – did five deliveries."

"You can give me a hand! This is my third delivery and I'm having twins!"

"Lead on." Jim said with a grin, as he followed Amy and Helen out the back of the shop to the living quarters. There they made Amy comfortable on a single bed. Amy sat sideways across the bed, with all the pillows and cushions they could find to support her at the back.

"Helen, have you got any gloves, and clean towels?"

"They are coming." Helen called as she ducked out of the room.

"Come here." Amy said to Terry, who was standing at the doorway, not certain what to do. She reached her hand out to him. Grateful, Terry came and sat next to Amy to hold her hand. Lizzie snuck in and sat next to Terry. As Helen came back with the towels which were put in place to protect the bed and wrap the babies, Jim put on the gloves and took a look how the labour was progressing.

"Are you ready to push yet?" Jim asked. "One of them is ready to come."

Amy nodded as she felt another contraction coming and concentrated on pushing. Once the contraction was over, she remembered her bag.

"Terry, can you open my case and get out the small red bag? Jim will need it once the twins are here."

Terry hastened to obey and put the bag next to Jim, while Amy waited for the next contraction to come.

"The next one should do it." Jim said as he opened the bag to get the scissors, clamps and string he needed.

"Is there anything I can get?" Helen called from the doorway. "I've called the doctor."

"Thank you. A big bowl of warm water would be good, once they have been delivered."

As the next contraction came, Amy gave the biggest push that she could.

"Now pant." Jim ordered her as the head emerged.

"Well done, the head's out!" Jim called. As they waiting for the baby to rotate, Helen came in. She had the local doctor who had come from the other end of town. As the next contraction came, Amy gave a final push for the baby to emerge. There was a couple of seconds when the doctor wiped the secretions from the baby's mouth and nose before it gave a gasp and cried.

"It's a Boy." Jim announced as the cord was clamped and tied, before it was cut and the baby wrapped in a towel. When he was handed to Amy, she immediately handed him to Terry.

"I still have work to do." She smiled.

Jim had a look. "This one's feet first! Doctor, I will let you do this one!" and immediately changed places.

Amy braced herself as another contraction came and began to push again.

"You made good progress with that one." The doctor told her as part of the body emerged.

"Try to do some more like that."

Amy obliged untill the doctor told her to pant. "We have just the head to deliver now. You have a daughter by the way." He frowned as he noticed the cord was across the neck. "Jim, hold the legs will you?" Jim quickly obeyed while the doctor grabbed the cord and moved it away from the baby's neck.

"I need to push!" Amy told him.

"A nice steady push." The doctor ordered as he guided the head through the passage.

There was an immediate gasp and cry once her head emerged. Once their daughter was wrapped and handed to Amy, she showed her to Terry, who was still engrossed with the son he never thought he would have.

Much later, when Amy's labour was safely completed, the twins had their first bath and check by the doctor before being dressed, fed and wrapped ready for travel. Helen brought in a couple of baby baskets and baby slings that she had acquired from other mothers in the settlement.

"I bet you haven't got anything with you to carry them in."

"No I haven't! We thought we had another fortnight! We wouldn't have made this trip if we had known! Thank you so much!"

Before Jim and James the Doctor left, Amy and Terry thanked them by having their son named after them. Their Daughter was to be Emily Helen. Helen was thrilled to have a twin named after her and made them promise to call in on the way home.

When the family finally emerged into the shop, it was crowded by local well-wishers who had come to see the twins.

"You must bring them in for a visit whenever you come through!" Helen ordered them.   "And send us some photos too!"

"We will." Amy and Terry promised. Lizzie hadn't been forgotten. She had been fed, watered and walked once it was noticed she was quietly sitting next to Terry.

It was late afternoon when the tired but happy family reached the motel.  The receptionist beamed and fussed over the new arrivals and gasped when she heard that they had arrived on the journey.

"Do you want a couple of bassinettes?" she asked. "It will be much more comfortable for them for sleeping. We have a few in our store room."

The bassinettes were accepted gratefully.  The motel owner came to set them up and also offered to bring in Dinner and breakfast for them which was also accepted.

When Terry called Lucy, she was immediately concerned.

"Terry! Is everything okay?  How's Mum?"

Terry couldn't keep the smile out of his voice. "She is fine.  She is just a little tired after delivering the twins!  You have a brother and a sister."

"I can't wait to get home on the weekend to see them!"

"You can see them tomorrow.  On our way over to see you, we had a little stop at Arthur's Pass where they decided to be born."

"No!"

"Yes!  We are at the motel in Christchurch."

"I will see you about two."

When she finished the call, any thought of study for the rest of the evening went out of the window.  Lucy turned to her friends with excitement.

"I've just been made an older sister to twins! Has anyone got any wool and be able to teach me some crochet?"

# LUCY AND HOANI

It took some months to finalise the sale of Hori and Kohi's house, and to get the plans for the shed approved before work could be started. It took another eighteen months for all the changes to the shed to be completed.

Lucy had only six weeks of practice with the Hokitika vet to do, to complete her training, when she came home one Friday afternoon. Her final exam had finished by lunchtime. As Lucy drove over the pass, she was glad that she would only have to make this journey one more time – to collect her certificate and badge at her passing out ceremony. The previous week Kohi had mentioned that they would have a little celebration when she came home after her exams.

When Lucy drove up the drive, she noticed both Terry and Frank's cars were there, among several cars she recognised from the pa. Lucy realised straight away that a much larger celebration was being organised! She saw the men standing around some sacks in the paddock and knew that a Hangi had been put down.

Hoani came running to meet Lucy as she parked and wrapped her in his arms. She noticed that he was wearing traditional dress.

"No more separations! It's wonderful to have you home at last!"

"What are we celebrating?" Lucy wanted to know.

"I will tell you shortly. Come with me."

With a little smile, Hoani led Lucy into the house by the lounge, instead of to the kitchen where Kohi was organising all the ladies with the remainder of the food.

He took Lucy to the room she shared with Reka. She noticed that a feather cloak was waiting on the bed.

Hoani turned Lucy to him and took her into his arms.

"We are celebrating not only you finishing your course, but the iwi are formally welcoming you into our family as my wife." Hoani looked at Lucy's astonished expression. "We will of course have a normal wedding and also there will be a formal presentation to the tribe at the pa. Are you ready for it? We can always delay the welcome till later if you aren't."

Lucy managed to get over her surprise and gave Hoani a radiant smile.

"I'm ready! We have waited so long for this day, and now it is here!"

Hoani and Lucy embraced untill the sound of footsteps forced them to part. Although she looked calm, Lucy's heart was fluttering at the knowledge that tonight they would be beginning their life together, and sharing their bed as a couple at last.

"Do I put this on now, or later?" Lucy asked, as she stroked the cloak.

"It's a Korowai. We will be giving them to each other later, in the ceremony. I wanted you to see it."

"Lucy! You are here! I see Hoani sneaked you in!" Kohi exclaimed as she came in the room to give Lucy a cuddle. She too was in traditional dress.

"He was showing me this beautiful Korowai cloak!" Lucy explained.

"Hoani, go and tell the men we are nearly ready." Kohi ordered him.

Kohi had a rummage in the wardrobe that Reka and Lucy shared, and brought out a white dress of Reka's.

"Will this fit you?"

Lucy slipped it on. It was a little short, but otherwise fitted. Kohi then lead Lucy out to the kitchen where she was reunited with her mother and the rest of the ladies. Reka grinned at the sight of Lucy in her dress. Lucy could see that she and Hoani weren't going to have any more time alone together untill formalities were over. She now understood why Hoani took her into the house through the lounge. Then Lucy heard a woman's voice calling Lucy and her family to come. Kohi, Reka and the ladies from the pa led Lucy and all of her family out to Lucy and Hoani's new home.

Claire and her girls were looking after the twins for the evening. The whole building had been transformed, from the Shed into a home upstairs, with multiple use areas down stairs. The open area was now set up with a long table for a banquet. There, Hoani and Hori were waiting, with the iwi standing in front.

Hoani and Lucy were then brought together for their troth. The cloaks were brought out for them to place over each-others' shoulders, before the declaration that they were married. The traditional hongi greetings were carried out between the couple and all the guests, before the Banquet followed, with celebrations carrying on till late over in Amy's old house.

After the banquet, Claire brought the children over to Amy and Terry. They were happy to retreat with them upstairs to one of the spare rooms where they would be sleeping with them overnight. Myrtle and Frank were to stay overnight as well. When Lucy and Hoani retired for the night and settled into bed, she turned to him with a happy sigh.

"This has been lovely, but when we have our civil wedding, I want a smaller celebration!"

"I completely agree!" Hoani said as he snuggled into her. "When are we going to have it?"

"As soon as we can arrange it."

"How about out at the bach? Do you want the vicar or a celebrant?"

"The bach will be lovely, and I think the celebrant will be best. We can choose our own vows."

"Are you going to wear that gorgeous dress again?"

Lucy looked at him in mock horror. "Brides are supposed to wear white at their first wedding!"

"You had that tonight!" Hoani grinned.

"That's true!" Lucy thought for a few seconds. "If you want to see me in it again, then that's what I will wear. What are you going to wear? – a suit or one of your grass skirts?"

Hoani's roar of laughter was heard at the other end of the house, which made them grin.

"I will surprise you!"

Lucy almost wished she hadn't suggested the skirt. She was having visions of him in a tux with a skirt instead of trousers.

The next morning Lucy woke with the morning light penetrating their room. She realised that she might be starting their family a little earlier than she expected. Not that it mattered, though if she was to wear the pink dress for their civil wedding, she needed to organise it sooner than later!

At breakfast time, Lucy was grateful that someone had stocked their fridge for them, as they had a full house. Frank and Myrtle, along with Terry and Amy stayed for the meal.

The twins were running around and full of mischief, exploring Lucy and Hoani's cupboards. When Hori and Kohi saw the curtains and blinds open in Hoani and Lucy's quarters, they also brought Reka over to join in the family breakfast.

Lucy was clearing up, when she received a call from the vet, wanting to know when she was available to help in the surgery. Hoani had been keeping him informed of her progress and that she was coming home for her final practice.

"I take it you want me to come in today? What time?"

"Will you be able to make it for eleven?" I have several cases of surgery I need a hand with."

Lucy looked at her watch. "I will see you then."

"Is that the vet? Hoani asked.

"It is." Lucy confirmed. "He wants me in for eleven. We will be doing surgery for the afternoon." She gave him a little smile. "Can you find out when we can get our marriage licence?"

"There isn't any rush is there?"

"If you want me to wear that dress, there is!"

Hoani looked at Lucy in shock. "You mean you may be...." His words trailed off.

Lucy grinned at him. "It's the right time, so I could be!"


The next few months were busy ones for Lucy. Lucy was kept busy at the vets most days, helping with the clinics or with surgery sessions. A number of animals also came home with her to be cared for. Lucy was grateful that Micky and Kelly also regularly helped with the animals.

They were going to miss Mickey, who was soon going to start his nursing training in Christchurch. Kelly had found a position at the café in town, and was volunteering with the emergency services. She was excited to be attending a number of workshops and training sessions in coming months.

In between it all, a month after she came home, Lucy and Hoani and their families, made the trip out to the bach. With Kelly and Reka as her bridesmaids – they found similar dresses in apricot. Lucy was relieved that she still fitted into her pink dress, given the knowledge that their first child was already on the way. Micky also supported Hoani as Best Man. Both Hoani and Micky wore smart trousers and shirts. Hoani had on a shirt that was especially made for him with tribal symbols all over it. Lucy noticed that Amy's animal family also came to see her ceremony too, and made sure she gave them all a special smile.

Hoani also was finally ready to send his book off for publishing. In addition to his own notes, Hoani's library of texts of native plants was growing, along with texts on the human anatomy. A large chart of the human body now hung in his office space, with photos of plants and their uses surrounding it. He also had a cupboard full of native plants that he used regularly for his healing sessions.

Most of the time, Hoani visited patients in their homes, but occasionally they came to his office. So Hoani was surprised one afternoon to find a pakeha male in the waiting area with his regular patients. This male was wearing a suit. Hoani gave him a form to fill out his details as he took in his first patient. When Hoani took the new patient in to his office, he noticed that there were no details on the patient's form about his issues.

Hoani also noticed that the Patient was taking notice of everything in the office.

"How can I help you." Hoani asked, after introducing himself.

"I'm Doug, the manager of our medical practice in Greymouth. I've been hearing great things about you and am here to see if your healing can be incorporated into our practice. Out of interest, what are your credentials?"

"You may be disappointed to learn I don't have any formal education in my craft; though I did get ninety eight per cent in my Uni exams, and was set to study biology. However an accident put an end to that.

My father-in-Law started up the native plant nursery here at that time, so I got a job with him, looking after the plants. I happened to ask about medicinal plants, which is now a comprehensive section in our nursery.

One of my aunts at the pa is a healer. She has been passing her knowledge to me." Hoani indicated the rows of files in his bookcase. "This is all the information she has passed to me." He then dived into a box in the corner.

"This arrived today. I've been working on it since the nursery opened. We will be making it available to our customers."

He handed a copy to Doug. Doug had a quick flick through the pages, and at a glance he could see how comprehensive the book was.

"Where do you source the plants you use?" Doug wanted to know.

"Most of them we collect seeds from the bush and grow in the nursery." Hoani opened his cupboard.

"The ones that are suitable to dry before use, are stored here, but a few we have to keep as plants in the nursery and use them fresh."

"What about dosages?" Doug wanted to know.

Hoani brought out a file with an A to Z of plants he used and the dosages or weights of plants for each age group.

"Have you ever had any reactions to your treatment?" Doug wanted to know.

"No. If a topical medication is needed, I check first what other treatments if any they have used and also do a skin test. I also do a check of their health history and on occasion call their GP to see if they have any allergies they may have forgotten about.

For internal medications, I also take a look at their diet, which can give me clues that a certain treatment may not be suitable. In that case, I sent them back to their GP to see if they have a treatment that may be more suitable."

"You should have been a GP!" Doug said finally. You will fit in well at our practice. Have you considered going to one of the colleges for natural therapies for your certificate?"

Hoanie shook his head. "After the accident, I know I can't do intensive study. Besides, I have plenty to keep me busy here, with helping at the nursery, my current practice not to mention helping the wife with her animals." Hoani grinned. She's a vet nurse and brings home wildlife that are brought into the vets."

"I understand, but what if you were able to do your certificate at your own pace by correspondence?"

"You really want me to do that certificate! Don't you? How often do you want me to be at your clinic?"

"If you get your certificate, you can get a government provider number, which means the patient only pays the gap." Doug mentioned the amount Hoani would be paid per consultation. "We would want you for a weekly session to begin with. – you could always do teleconferencing of follow ups for your patients if needed in between time. What do you say?"

"I will have to have a think about it. Which is the best college to do the certificate through?"

"They have one in Christchurch. You would only have to go there for exams. Could you manage that?"

"I suppose so. My wife will be laughing that I've let myself in for this. She's not long finished two years of her course over there."

After Doug let himself out, Hoani sat in his office for several minutes, wondering whether he had done the right thing, putting extra pressure on himself when he had just achieved a comfortable pace and place in his life. After Hoani's consultations, he usually bounded upstairs to be with Lucy, so she wondered what was keeping him and came downstairs to find him lost in thought. She put a comforting hand on his shoulder.

"What is it?" Lucy asked gently.

Hoani put his hand over hers. "I hope I'm doing the right thing!" His voice was full of anxiety. Lucy hadn't heard that since he told her he wasn't going to University.

"What are we doing?" Lucy kissed and cuddled him as she spoke.

"The practice manager at the Greymouth GP clinic has been for a visit. He wants me to become part of their team – doing a session each week."

He stopped Lucy's gasp of amazement. "He wants me to do the Natural Therapies certificate!

They have a college in Christchurch. Apparently I can do it by correspondence, but will have to go over for exams!"

Lucy managed to suppress the laughter that was welling inside her. "That's wonderful! We will have to reorganise your schedule so you can do it, without stressing about other things."

"I still want to be in the plant nursery and do my healing consultations. I'm not sure just what I can reorganise."

"Well, you can leave the animals to me while your studying and reduce the number of days you do your consultations. Have at least one or two days a week that you devote to your study. After seeing all the study you've done to publish your book, I know you can do it!"

"Thank you for believing in me!" Hoani hugged her. He put his hand round her waist to rest it on her gently rounded stomach.

"He or she believes in you too!" Lucy added. Her expression full of her love and trust in him.

Hoani took Lucy in his arms for a kiss. He finally knew that his insecurities would no longer constrain him. That with Lucy's support he could do anything he wanted.

# REKA'S ENCOUNTER

On leaving school, Reka had found work doing cleaning duties at the rest home, while she decided what she wanted to do. She loved being with Amy and Terry's twins and Hoani and Lucy's daughter, Alice Kohia. Reka would have applied to be a Karitane Nurse, but that career path was no longer available. Then she considered being a Nanny. There was a course she could do, but it was in Auckland, well away from family and friends. While she was deciding what she would do, she made a visit to Moana out at the pa.

Hoani had dropped her off for her visit on his way to his session at the Greymouth GP clinic, promising to pick her up on his way home. Reka heard a car approaching. Thinking that it was Hoani, she had run out to the gate, only to find it wasn't Hoani, but a car full of youths from the pa.

Spotting a familiar face, Toby had stopped the car opposite her, to give her a smile and a wave. Toby had been in Reka's class at school. He hadn't seen her since their school days. The youth beside him invited her to go for a ride. Recognising Toby, she returned his smile. She had liked him at school, but wasn't ready for a serious relationship yet. The expectant grins on the other youths' faces told Reka that she would be getting more than a ride if she went with them.

"Thanks for the offer, but my brother is coming for me." Reka replied, before turning and heading back inside to wait with Moana. It was several minutes before the car moved on. If she had heard the conversation in the car, Reka would have been alarmed.

"Does anyone know who she is?" one asked.

"She's Reka. I went to school with her." Toby spoke. "You can keep your eyes off! I've spoken to the iwi. She's mine!"

"That's not happening!" spoke another. What belongs to one, belongs to us all! Remember that when you get patched."

For the first time, Toby had misgivings about joining the gang. He had no qualms about the activities the gang normally engaged in, moving stolen goods or dealing in drugs. He had been exposed to them since his older brother joined several years ago. It was taken for granted that Toby would join too. The fact that he was expected to share his woman, was something that Toby wasn't prepared for.

"We haven't had a GB for a while. When did you last have one, Toby?"

Toby was now alarmed, though he managed not to show it. He knew that GB was a gang bang. He didn't want them to know he was a virgin, or that taking part in a rape wasn't Toby's idea of fun either. He knew he was being tested, but how could he put them off?

"I haven't, but I have a Kereru to pluck for tonight."

"Who's that? Is it Reka?"

"No." Toby smiled that his ruse had worked. "Just a barmaid at the pub. Let me know when your next shipment is in. She wants to score."

As they discussed the coming shipment, Toby moved off, relieved that he (and Reka) had escaped their attention for now. After dropping the gang members off, Toby realised that if he wanted to avoid becoming part of the gang, he would have to move away! And also warn Reka that she was now a target of the gang.

Reka was in the lounge room with Hori and Kohi, discussing her future. She had spoken to Hoani about her plans. He had encouraged her to follow her dream of working with children.

"When you're done, you can always come and be a nanny for us!"

Reka had gone ahead and applied for a position on the Nanny training course. She was surprised and delighted to hear the next day that she had been accepted. While they were talking, a car came down the drive. She recognised Toby's car, wondering why he was here. She immediately got up to go to the door, her feeling of anxiety reflected in her face.

"Who is it?" Hori asked. He also got up, after noticing the anxiety on Reka's face. Reka turned to face her father.

"It's Toby from the pa. He and a carload of mates stopped when I was at Moana's yesterday. They offered me a ride, which of course I didn't accept. I'm wondering why he is here."

Hori steered Reka back to the couch next to Kohi.
"I will deal with this."

For several minutes, quiet conversation could be heard at the doorstep. Reka had expected her father to send Toby away, so both she and Kohi were surprised when Hori led Toby in and sat him in the chair next to Kohi while Hori sat on the other side of Reka.

"Does anyone know you are here?" Hori asked Toby.

I'm fairly sure I wasn't followed and made a couple of stops and detours to check no-one was tracking me." Toby then turned to Reka. "I'm sorry to come like this, Reka, but I know you're in danger now, and had to warn you."

Kohi put a protective arm around Reka and held her hand.

"Are you talking about your mates in the car?"

Toby nodded. "They aren't my mates!"

The family listened in silence while Toby's story came out, of how his brother was a member of a gang and that he now was expected to become part of it.

"I have already decided to leave the coast tonight, to make a new life for myself. I'm most concerned about Reka. After seeing her, I know they won't rest till they have...." Toby paused. He couldn't bring himself to say the words. So Reka said them for him.

"You mean they intend to rape me?"

Toby nodded miserably.

"I could tell that when I saw them." Reka looked at her parents. "It's just as well then, that I'm moving away as well."

"Yes." Hori's tone was firm. "We will be taking you away tonight. Go and pack your bags!" He looked at Toby. "Which direction are you heading?"

"South."

"We won't say where we are heading, just in case someone tries to get it out of you." Hori declared. Toby nodded his agreement.

As Reka stood up, Toby also stood up. She walked over to him and put her hand in his. As she did, a little tingle went through her fingers, making her smile as she looked at their hands. She then looked into his eyes.

"Thank you for coming. It may be some time, but we will catch up again." She thought for a second or two, "I will get your number." Reka fetched her phone and entered Toby's number. "Take care." Reka said in parting before she left the room to pack.

Hori and Kohi had also stood up. "I will see you out." Hori said, distracting Toby from his gaze of Reka as she left the room.

"Thanks." Toby replied as he followed Hori out. He was thankful Reka hadn't said goodbye and the fact that she was keeping in touch with him, helped to sustain him in the many months to come while they were apart.

"I would head south the back way, if I was you." Hori advised Toby. "Keep going out the Kaniere road and cross the Kaniere bridge for Rimu." Hori paused before adding "If you really want to disappear, I would get rid of that car as soon as you can, same with your phone! Send a letter to Reka with your new number and we will pass it on. You may also need a new name."

Toby thought for a few moments.

"If you had another son, what would you have called him?"

"Kiwa."

Toby smiled. "That's Guardian of the Ocean. Kiwa is who I will be."

Toby reached for a Pounamu taonga in the shape of a bird that was hanging around his neck.

"Can you get the iwi to give this to the family?"

"I will." Hori accepted the pendant, knowing that this act formally cut Toby off completely. That he would no longer be regarded as part of his family.

"Thanks again." Toby said in parting.

As Hori watched Toby's car head down the drive, Hoani came out.

"Is everything okay?"

"No. Reka is in danger of being gang raped. We are taking her to safety tonight.

I will be away for a week. Kohi will stay with her till she is settled. I want you to lock the gate after us and install some decent security cameras in case they come around here! Be prepared to defend yourselves!" the upset and anger in Hori's voice was plain.

"Who was that?" Hoani asked with concern, at the situation they were now in.

"That was Toby, a friend of Reka's from the pa. He came to warn us. He is in danger too. They will probably try to kill him. If you see the iwi before me, can you give Toby's Taonga to them to pass it his family? He is changing his name as well. It would be best if you don't go near the pa for a bit, though I'm worried about Moana."

"Why is Moana in danger?" Hoani's alarm was growing.

"Reka was at Moana's place when the gang saw her. They will try to get out of her where Reka lives."

Hoani made his mind up. "I'm going to get Moana out of there!"

"Then be very careful!" Hori gave Hoani a cuddle before he returned to the house to prepare for the journey. By now Lucy had come downstairs to see what was happening.

"You're not going alone!" Lucy was adamant when she was told of the situation. "I will ring Mum and leave Alice with her."

They both raced upstairs. Lucy to call Amy and Hoani called Moana.

"Are you okay Moana?"

"I'm fine. What's wrong?" She knew that this wasn't a social call at this hour.

"You're in danger, there. We are coming to pick you up."

132

"Who from?"

"The Gang. I will explain later. Just be ready to leave when we come."

Moana knew Hoani wouldn't be doing this without very good reason. She looked around her. What to take? She had been here for most of her adult life. She went to her wardrobe and pulled out her bag. When Hoani arrived, he also had Lucy and Terry with him. Moana had her bag and several boxes ready to take. Within five minutes, they were ready to leave. Moana deliberately left her front door open. She didn't want it to be damaged when people inevitably came to see where she was. Her neighbour Tui came out as they were packing the car.

"Are you coming back?" Tui asked Moana.

"I don't know. It won't be for a long time if I do." Moana looked at Tui with tears in her eyes. "It isn't safe for me here now."

"Who from?" Tui's tone hardened that this was happening to her friend from school days.

"The gang." Moana's answer was to the point. She gave Tui a cuddle before she joined the family in the car.

After Moana left, Tui went through the house, removing every valuable item she could find, to keep for her friend, in case she came back. She also decided to have a word with the iwi! What was the place coming to, when elder members of the community didn't feel safe there anymore!

During the next few days, there was plenty to gossip about at the pa. Word spread that Moana had moved out and that Toby was missing. The iwi visited the Kaniere Road property where Hoani lived, to find the gate locked and a security system installed.

They realised the situation was much more serious than they had envisaged.     It was only after they called Hoani, that he came to let them in and advised them of the changed circumstances.   They shook their heads when Hoani give them the Pounamu Taonga.   It was unheard of for a tribe member to cut themselves off like this.

When Hori's car pulled out of the drive, The boot was full of clothes and items that Reka would be needing for her studies, while she was away.

"I know you can't sleep Reka, but it would be best for you to lie down untill we get past Greymouth. Make yourself as comfy as you can." Hori instructed her. Reka was glad she had brought her pillow and a favourite rug from her bed. To begin with, thoughts of both Toby, and her future away from her family, filled her head. Despite herself, she nodded off to sleep.

Hori was concerned that when they passed the pa, a car came out and followed them, but peeled off at the turn off for the Cobden Bridge. Another car continued to follow them through to Nelson. Hori stopped at a twenty four hour service station for fuel. He made sure he locked the car while outside. Luckily Reka had slept till now. When she awoke the car was stopped and both her mother's coat and her father's jacket were covering her.

"Are we being followed Mum?" Reka spoke through the blankets and clothes. Kohi pretended to yawn and covered her mouth as she replied.

"Yes. Don't move!"

The following car had also stopped there for fuel. Kohi didn't look at them, but knew they were taking a good look at the contents of their car.

As Hori waited to pay, he heard someone come in behind him. He turned his head. It was Ben, Toby's brother. Hori nodded his head to acknowledge him then turned back to face the register.

"You're travelling late." Ben spoke.

Hori turned to face him. "We are hoping to get the first ferry in the morning. We're heading up to see Kohi's brother. He isn't well, so we are going to see him in case he doesn't make it."

"Your kids aren't coming?"

"Not as this stage. they both have jobs to stay for. We can call them to come for the funeral if need be."

"You didn't bother flying up?"

"No. We would have needed to hire a car. We don't know at this stage how long we need to be there, and given that it will only take a day or so to get up there in our car, it made sense to take our own."

"Next please!" Hori was grateful the station attendant interrupted their conversation.

Hori gave Ben another nod as he passed him before returning to the car. Three youths that Hori suspected were also gang members were standing by Hori's car as he returned.

"Going on holiday?" one asked.

"Not quite." Hori replied. The wife's brother isn't well. We are heading over to see him. We don't know at this stage how long we need to be there. As you can see, we are prepared for a longish stay."

"You always lock your doors?" one asked as Hori unlocked the car.

"Always! Don't you? You never know who would be poking around and pinching your stuff."

"Like who?"

Hori gave him a scornful look. "The cops for a start!"

This drew a peal of laughter from them.

"Too true, Bro."

Hori was relieved that they moved away as Ben came out to join them. He swiftly entered the car and drove away before they tried to detain him on any other excuse.

Hori was relieved that Ben and his mates didn't try to follow them to Picton and that they were able to get the first ferry to Wellington. However, just to be safe, Reka retreated under the blanket and jackets when it came time to disembark from the ferry.

Hori was relieved that he managed to get a few hours' sleep in Picton and a couple more on the ferry over the strait. As the drive up to Auckland was a very long twelve hours, a stop overnight at New Plymouth was called for and a walk in Pukekura Park helped to stretch their legs.

In Auckland, they settled into a Remuera motel. Both Reka and Kohi were surprised at how hilly Auckland was. Reka had visions of hard work, pushing prams on the hills here! They treated themselves to dinner in the city and a visit to the Sky tower to see the night lights come on around the harbour.

The next morning they took Reka to the Nanny training school, where she was given forms to fill in, given her timetables and shown her accommodation. There was to be a two day introduction to the college before the classes started. Reka noticed she wasn't the only student who had arrived early. She exchanged smiles with them as they passed in the corridor. One stopped and introduced herself.

"I'm Mahina. Will you be with us for lunch?"

Reka looked at Hori and Kohi. They nodded and smiled. It was obvious that she was going to be making friends and be looked after here.

"We will bring your things, and then we will let you settle in." Kohi told her. "We will pop in tomorrow to see you before we head back to the coast."

When Hori and Kohi returned, Reka had a big beam on her face.

"I'm going to miss you, but I can see I will have a great time here. Don't worry about me."

"Make sure you keep your phone topped up and charged as we will be calling you in the evenings, once we get home. I told Toby to write once he gets his new phone and we will pass it on to you. He is also changing his name to Kiwa."

"Thanks Dad." Reka replied. Giving them both a hug. She hadn't spoken about it, but she was deeply worried at how Toby was going. "Shouldn't I be getting a new phone too? I will use your mothers' names. Kiri Pania Tahini." Hori nodded at the wisdom of Reka's suggestion.

After her parents had departed, Reka changed Toby's details to Kiwa. She also popped out to the shops for another phone. By the time they reached New Plymouth, a message from Kiri was waiting on Hori's phone.

Hoani was surprised when Hori called to be let in the gate a day early and Kohi was with him.

"It went well then?" Hoani asked after they followed him up the stairs and were reunited with Lucy and Moana.

"Apart from the gang escort behind us all the way to Nelson. Reka is settled and happy at the college. How have things been here?"

"The iwi have been for a visit and have given Toby's family his Taonga. I've been busy at the practice at Greymouth too."

At the pa, Toby's family had a meeting. Toby's Taonga was on the table in front of them. His mother looked at Ben. "You know what you have to do!"

"I'm already onto it!"

# TOBY'S FLIGHT TO SAFETY

As Toby approached Kaniere, he stopped at the township. The sim was removed from his phone, which was ditched.

The sim was buried in the forest on his journey. Toby stayed the night at Fox Glacier, before refuelling and heading through to Queenstown. It was a long day's drive, but he still didn't feel completely safe.

In Queenstown, Toby picked up a new phone and looked through southern newspapers for job ads. There was one looking for crew on a fishing boat at bluff. He would contact them tomorrow. The next day Toby was up early for the trip to Invercargill where he visited the car scrap yard.

"Are you sure you want it scrapped? I can see it is too good for that!"

"I need it to "disappear!"

"What's it been used for?"

"It hasn't been used for anything. I don't want it traced to where I am."

"What are you running from?"

"A gang. I was supposed to be patched, but they wanted to gang rape my girl, so we split. I know they will kill me if they can."

"They shouldn't trace you to here."

"They can trace my car anywhere. The enforcer has a brother in the police."

"What if it is given a paint job, new plates and sent overseas? I know there are buyers who will pay good money for this."

"Okay then, but just make sure it can't be traced back to me."

Toby was given enough cash to buy an old Vauxhall that he had seen for sale on a front lawn. A call to the fishing boat resulted in Toby getting a trial on the fishing boat. It was leaving port that evening. Toby made a trip to the shops for work clobber, before he headed for Bluff.

A look round Bluff, which was a much smaller settlement than Invercargill, showed Toby that he needed to find somewhere to live in Invercargill. This suited him, as it would be much easier to be anonymous there.

For the first week though, Toby had to sleep in the car untill he was paid and had sufficient funds to find a flat. Packets of hygiene wipes allowed Toby to pass muster untill he was able to have his first shower. During that week Toby sent his first letter to his new family. He also filled in a form to change his name to Kiwa Tahini. Setting up a bank account with his new identity was a challenge, but with perseverance, Kiwa was happy to see his new card come in the mail. He also resat his driving licence with his new name.

When Hori received Kiwa's letter, there were smiles and chuckles at the contents. When he passed it to Kohi, Hori gave a sigh of relief.

"He's going to be okay."

Once Kiwa adjusted to being on the ocean, he enjoy his time at sea and quickly learnt the various tasks he was expected to do when they were on the fishing grounds. Kiwa knew that this job was only temporary as the season was for only six months. He would have to find another job at the end of the season.

Some of the regular boat crew managed to survive the following six months by living frugally, but Kiwa wanted to build his funds while he could.

He had never had a proper job before and enjoyed the security that a healthy bank account gave him.

During the last week of the season, a new hand was brought onto the boat when one of the regulars was off sick. As soon as Kiwa saw the tattoos the new hand was wearing, he knew trouble was here! Kiwa recognised a fully patched gang member when he saw one. During the voyage, he spotted the new member looking at him quizzically and at one point was flicking through his phone, even though they were out of range of phone reception. Kiwa's blood ran cold when a voice behind him called to him.

"Hey Toby! Come and help with this net."

Kiwa managed to not react or hear the call and moved away to another part of the deck to help one of the other crew. Kiwa turned around to find the new hand now in his face and was angry.

"Toby! I told you to help me with the net!"

Kiwa allowed himself to be equally angry.

"My name's NOT Toby! You keep calling me that, and you can do it all yourself!" Kiwa growled as he started to started to make his way to the nets. The new hand shoved the phone with Toby's photo in his face.

"You're Toby!" the new hand insisted.

Kiwa took a glance at the photo and gave the hand a dismissive look as he swiped the phone to the floor. Kiwa saw with some satisfaction that the phone fell apart and got wet as a wave swept across the deck. The new hand scrambling to grab the phone before it was lost overboard. He wouldn't be using it again this trip!

"I don't care a f... whether I look like your Toby!" Kiwa shouted at him. "If you insist on calling me Toby, both you and your precious phone will end up in the ocean! Get someone else to help you with the nets!"

Kiwa stomped off for a comfort stop. Everyone on the deck and Doug the skipper in the wheelhouse stopped to watch the exchange. They had never seen Kiwa angry before. When Kiwa came back out, Doug called him over for a chat.

"Is everything okay?'

"No. That wanker is insisting that I'm someone called Toby. I have no idea who or what Toby is, but I had pleasure in threatening to throw both him and his precious phone in the ocean!" Kiwa sighed. "I presume he's going to be on here for the rest of the week?"

Doug nodded.

"In that case, we will make this trip my last."

"We will miss you." Doug said, internally sighing that he had to find another crew member for the last few days.

Back at the dock, it was usual to go for a beer at the pub, but this time Kiwa went straight to his car.

"You're not joining us?" Kev one of the regulars came and asked him.

"Not today. I will catch you later."

"That walley has got you on the run! Hasn't he?" A flicker of fear in Kiwa's eyes told him he was right. "Take care! It's been great to have you with us." Kev shook Kiwa's hand.

"It's been great to be with you all too. Have one for me!"

As Kiwa drove away, he noticed that the new hand had joined Kev.

Kiwa knew that the details of his car were being noted. Back at Invercargill, Kiwa picked up some groceries and topped his car with fuel. It was time for him to move on.

Kiwa made a trip to the hardware shop for a car cover and to the bike shop for a cheap bike; before heading to his unit to finish packing up. He had kept it clean and tidy. In half an hour, he was ready to leave and dropped off the key to the Real Estate agent.

On the road, Kiwa was glad that he had already organised his next job for when he finished this one. This meant that he had a few extra days break before he was expected. Kiwa's destination was only a few hours away, at Manapouri. Pouring rain had set in when he turned in the drive of the Lodge. Low cloud and the rain hid most of the vast lake opposite. Kiwa was grateful for being able to access his room early. He chose a quieter room at the back of the complex, where his car wouldn't be noticed as much. Kiwa was also happy that the café bar area was open, so didn't have to go out in the wet again, to enjoy a few beers with his meal. He was feeling tired after being up all night and then travelling here. Sleeping at night again was another thing Kiwa was looking forward to.

Back in his room, Kiwa messaged Reka. It took him time to get used to calling her Kiri, just as she had to adjust to calling him Kiwa. She didn't answer straight away, so Kiwa found himself dozing off while he waited for the messages on his phone to ping. When she answered his message, he was sound asleep, so it was the next morning before Kiwa found her message, that she was flying to Christchurch urgently. Hori was in hospital with a suspected heart attack!

Kiwa cursed the position he was in! He wanted to drop everything and head for Christchurch, regardless of the danger he was going into. He realised though, that by the time he got there, Hori would probably be treated and be on his way home to the coast.

Reka realised when Kiwa didn't answer her message, that he was probably asleep, so she was ready when her phone rang the next morning. She, along with Kohi and Moana were at Hori's bedside, where he was resting comfortably after a session in the cardiac catheter lab to have some stents inserted into his blocked arteries.

"Rek..Kiri! Is Hori okay?" Kiwa's panicked tones came down the phone as Reka quickly exited the room.

"Calm down Love!" Reka's soothing voice answered him. Did he detect more maturity in her voice? It was obvious that her training was having an effect. "Dad has had some stents put in and he is resting now. They intend to send him back to the coast tomorrow."

"Will you be going over?"

"No. I will go straight back to my training. They were kind enough to give me a couple of days to visit." Just then Kohi was at the door asking if that was Kiwa on the phone. Reka nodded. Hori wanted to talk to him.

"Hi Hori, how are you feeling?"

"Much better than yesterday! How's things your way?'

"I had an interesting day yesterday. Some walley tried to rumble me! His phone nearly went in the drink! He was lucky he didn't go in too!"

"Is he...?"

"Yep! When I saw his tatts, I knew trouble was here! I've moved, with a new job next week. I was going to come!"

"No need, but thanks anyway. Keep your head down and keep in touch."

"I will do! It's time you took care of yourself instead of us!"

144

Hori had to smile as he handed the phone back to Reka. Kiwa was right. There had been so many stressful events for him to cope with, this year, it was no wonder that he had this heart attack. He knew it was time he took stock of his life and made some changes.

At Manapouri, Kiwa looked out the window. It was pouring with rain again. He had acclimatised to working in these conditions on the boat. At least with his position as a labourer for the local builder, he didn't have to cope with a moving deck and seasickness.

The first day on the boat, Kiwi spent half the time with his head over the side. He didn't dare go below, but just kept going when he wasn't being sick. On their return to the dock, there were lots of grins among the crew.

"Will we see you tonight?" Doug the skipper asked.

"Of course!" Kiwa managed a grin. "Hopefully there will be less berley for the fish!"

"Come with us! You've earnt a feed and a beer!"

Kiwa fetched his wet gear from the boot of the car for his walk. Kiwa's first stop was at reception to ask where people usually stay when here long term.

"We have two caravan and camping parks. Most people stay at them." On a map of the town, she circled the lodge, the parks and the supermarket. "Here's the local hall. We have all sorts of activities on there. There's something to keep you busy almost every night of the week if you want."

Kiwa visited both of the camping parks. He noticed that one had more permanent occupants than the other. It was also further from the facilities than the other park.

Kiwa popped in for a chat to reception. When he left, he had seen the vans and chalets available for long term stays and had booked in for six months with an option for longer. Kiwa was checking out the supermarket when a call came from Les the builder, enquiring whether he was still coming.

"I'm already here." Kiwa told Les. "I finished the other job yesterday, so came a few days early."

"I thought you were finishing there on Friday?"

Kiwa decided to tell the truth. "I was, but a bloke from a gang came on the boat and was causing trouble. I decided it wasn't worth staying the extra few days and moved on."

"Are you in a Gang?" Les correctly read in between the lines that the gang member was causing Kiwa trouble.

"No, but my brother is. He's over on the West Coast. I was supposed to be patched too, but the gang members made it clear they would be having sex with my girlfriend whether she agreed or not."

"Is she with you?"

"No. She is on a Nanny training course in Auckland."

"What do her family say about all this?"

"Like me, they weren't impressed. When I warned them, they took her away to safety. Before I left, her father gave me some tips on how to disappear, which have worked till now."

"Who was your skipper on the boat?"

"Doug, on the Neptune."

"I know him. I will call you back about next week."

"Okay." Kiwa knew that Les's call to Doug would decide whether he had work with him or not.

146

Kiwa didn't blame him. No-one wanted employees that came with potential trouble by gangs.

Kiwa took a walk to the local hall. At the entrance was a noticeboard with a number of notices of activities on there. Among them Kiwa noticed one for martial arts. It occurred to Kiwa it would be a handy skill for him to have.

When Les rang him back saying the job wasn't available any longer, Kiwa was philosophical about it and thanked him for his time. Les was feeling guilt at letting Kiwa go. Doug had told him to look after Kiwa as he was one of the best crew he had on his boat. Les still wasn't happy that here was someone with links to a gang, no matter that he wasn't in it.

As Kiwa walked along the waterfront, both the wind and the rain were easing. He decided then, that he was going to stay. It was a nice little community here. If he was careful with his money, he could last six months here easily. Kiwa wondered about other jobs locally and took a walk back to the community notice board at the supermarket. There were dog walkers and other tradies, but no gardeners or handy men there. Kiwa had found his niche.

Les had expected Kiwa to disappear from the area in a few days, so he was surprised to hear that Kiwa had started up a little business in the town, that kept him busy in the months to come.

When Kiwa attended his first session at the hall, there was not one but several classes to choose from. Judo karate and jujitsu. He decided to try them all.

Although Kiwa appreciated the fitness that came with the physical training at the classes, what he enjoyed the most was the socialising afterwards.

Kiwa learnt that some of the men also liked to go fishing. Once they heard he had been on a fishing trawler, Kiwa soon found himself invited on fishing trips. Apart from missing Reka, Kiwa's life was full.

# KIDNAPPED!

In the months after Kiwa left the West Coast, his brother Ben and other gang members were flummoxed that his younger brother had not only left without a word, but had succeeded in disappearing. He had stopped using his phone, his car had vanished, and he hadn't used his bank account either. There was only one thing for it, they spread the word through all the gangs in the country. Every gang member had a photo of Toby with an instruction to eliminate him.

They also tried to target Reka. On the evening that Toby disappeared, Ben saw Hori's car and decided to follow him, not realising that Reka was being spirited out under their noses. On their return to the pa, they visited Moana's house, but she had moved out. Ben knew that Hori's family lived out Kaniere road, but found another family was living in his house and they didn't know where he now lived. There was no sign of Reka around town, so they took it that Reka was hiding with Toby.

It wasn't untill six months later, that the gang was given a lead to Toby's location. A gang member from Invercargill swore he worked with Toby on a trawler from Bluff. The bloke called himself Kiwa, but was the spitting image of Toby. The informant also gave a car registration. Fortunately for Kiwa, Luke the enforcer's brother was no longer in the police. He had been stood down after being caught accessing information he wasn't authorised to. The gang now knew that Kiwa was somewhere in the south. It was only a matter of time before they found him.

It took a television news item in Auckland, the camera sweeping Queen Street, that showed the gang that Kiwa and Reka were apart. In the scene Reka and Mahina were talking and smiling together as they were out shopping, completely oblivious to the fact that they were being filmed. Neither Ben, Kiwa or Hori's family saw the news item, but one of the other gang members did, and rang Ben immediately, advising him that Reka was in Auckland. Ben then contacted gang members in Auckland, asking them to find her. The gang in Invercargill were also asked to do a search of all towns in Southland and Fiordland to find him.

Finding Reka turned out to be relatively simple. Reka's friend Mahina was the sister of Kawa, a gang leader who had seen the news item. He grinned to see his sister on the TV news. He knew that his sister had made a new friend, Reka Tahini at their training college, and guessed correctly that the girl with Mahina was Reka. When word came through that Reka Tahini was to be located, they were able to send word back they had her location. A watch was put on the college to find out what room she was sleeping in. When that was established, they looked at entrances to the building, cameras and the routine of security there.

When the call finally came to "snatch Reka," the gang had a plan in place. What they hadn't planned on, was the presence of Mahina.

It was Thursday evening and Reka was doing her homework. Light was fading, so Reka pulled down the blinds at the window, which delighted the gang. There wouldn't be anyone outside to witness the kidnap. Mahina had her blind down too, so they couldn't see that she had moved from her room to Reka's to do their homework together.

Once darkness set in, the gang made their move. Outside the accommodation block a dark van drew up. Security wasn't due round yet and the accommodation block wasn't due to be locked for another hour. Dressed in dark clothing, with gloves and balaclavas' they slipped into the building and made their way up the fire escape. They had to wait several minutes as girls came and went from their rooms. Once it became quiet again they swiftly moved to Reka's door. The door knob was tested. It was unlocked. A nod was given.

Out of the corner of her eye, Mahina saw a flash of movement by the door as the lights went out in the room. She grabbed Reka and held her tight as she realised what was happening. The sound of swift movement of feet across the room then a strong smelling rag was put over their faces. As awareness faded, Reka and Mahina could feel themselves being wrapped up in a blanket. The gang member tasked with carrying Reka out of the building didn't expect her to be so heavy, so he struggled as he carried them down the stairs. Luck was with the gang as they reached the entrance. They exited the building and within a minute, the girls were bundled into the van. The van drew smoothly away as if they were normal visitors.

There was silence in the van as it negotiated back roads to a warehouse. The blanket was kept in place over the girls' bodies. It would be easier to control her if she started to struggle. Chloroform was kept handy in case Reka started to wake up again. They didn't want her to be awake untill they were nearer their destination. Inside the warehouse, a large hoist was waiting for the van to reverse onto, before being elevated to the back of a large truck.

Some large boxes were packed into the truck to hide the van, before the doors were shut and the truck made its way to the motorway south.

Hori had already called Reka earlier in the evening and Kiwa had already exchanged texts with her before the raid was made. By the time Hori received the call from the college the next morning that Reka was missing, the truck was being loaded on the inter-Island ferry. Mahina's parents were also receiving the same call. Questions were being asked whether they had stayed out overnight, but when they searched Reka's room, it was in disarray, with both Reka and Mahina's books left open. There was a distinct smell in the room, that the police later identified as chloroform. They now knew that the girls had been abducted. The Hokitika police were called and asked to interview Hori.

When Hori received the call from the college, he knew what had happened and where Reka was being taken. He made a call to Kiwa.

"I've got bad news mate. I've just had a call that Reka is missing. It can only mean that they know where you are too! Exactly where are you? We need to tell the police so they can be ready to intervene when they bring Reka your way."

There was a gasp from Kiwa and the sound of sobbing as he knew what was coming. Through the sobs, Kiwa managed to tell him. "I'm at the Manapouri camping ground." before he ended the call.

Hori then called the Hokitika Police.

"We were just about to come and talk to you. What can you tell us?"

Under the blanket, Reka put her hand in Mahina's and gave it a gentle squeeze. She squeezed Reka's hand back. They could feel the movement of the boat underneath them. The deep sound of the ferry's engines could also be heard. Whatever lay ahead, they were in it together.

Kawa's phone rang. It was their mother. Everyone in the van could hear her. She sounded both upset and angry.

"Do you know where Mahina and Reka are?"

"They are at the college, aren't they?" Kawa glanced at the bundle on the floor at the back. As he looked, he realised that the bundle was too big for one girl's body.

"They've been kidnapped! Find out what's going on!"

"I will do!" Kawa ended the call. As he stared at the bundle in the back, he was racking his brains what to do about Mahina. Delivering people between gangs was part and parcel of their code, with no questions asked. But this time, his sister was caught up in it. He realised that this outing was not going to end the way they had expected. He had a feeling the girls were already awake, but were keeping quiet for now, which suited him. The longer they lay still, the more time he had to think of a solution.

"Is everything okay?" the driver beside Kawa saw him give the bundle a good stare. He too had heard that Kawa's sister was missing.

"Just checking she's still asleep." Kawa forced himself to face away from the girls.

"You don't think...."

"We will sort it later if she is."

"I need a pee soon." One of the gang complained as the sound of vehicles started around them, in preparation to disembark.

"We all need one. We will have to wait till we get off this and go somewhere quiet."

The truck drove off the ferry and headed for some warehouses on the edge of the terminal. Inside the warehouse, the occupants of the van were relieved when they were hoisted from the truck. They parked in a corner near the office where a security guard was sitting. Kawa got out and spoke to the guard, who waved him to the conveniences. Kawa came to the back of the van and slapped the blanket as he called to his mates.

"Everyone out. The toilet is to the right."

Slowly Mahina and Reka moved the blanket from over them and gingerly moved themselves across the floor of the van to step out into the warehouse. Kawa pointed to the toilet; his face was impassive. Both of the girls wore quiet but determined expressions as they joined the queue. When it came to their turn, Mahina grabbed Reka's hand and took her in with her.

"There's no need..." Kawa began. Mahina gave him a withering look as she shut the door. Before they went outside, they had a cuddle.

"Be strong." Mahina urged Reka.

"I can now, but I know what's coming."

"What is coming?"

"Being gang raped in front of my boyfriend, before they kill him."

Back in the van, Mahina and Reka sat quietly on one of the seats at the back. A gang member sat either side of them.

The next stop was at a drive through for some breakfast, before they started the drive south. As they drove out through the hills south of Nelson, Kawa made a call.

"Ben, we are south of Nelson."

"You have the goods?"

"Yes."

"Call me when you reach Te Anau. Feel free to use her on the way. She is to be stripped and her clothes disposed of before the meet."

"Understood." Kawa disconnected the call before Ben could issue any more instructions.

Mahina looked at Reka with horror and cuddled her. It was obvious that the gang intended to do more than rape her. Mahina could feel rage welling up inside her! She had to do something to stop her friend being killed!

Reka could see the anger and determination in Mahina's face. She had to try to calm her. To cover her own panic, Reka squeezed Mahina's hand. Her voice came with a calmness she didn't know she possessed.

"Mahina love, there is nothing you can do about what is coming for me. At some point we will be separated, as I know your brother won't be allowing you to be with me for the end. I'm just glad you have been here to help me get through this part of my ordeal. We can only make the most of the time we have left."

There was silence in the van as they continued on their way to the West Coast. Kawa was glad Reka had mentioned the subject that he had been wrestling with – separating her from Mahina. He could now plan what he had to do.

Finally Mahina gave a big sigh as she accepted Reka's words and surprised everyone with her own.

"You know," Mahina began in a laconic way, "losing your virginity isn't all it's cracked up to be!"

Reka gasped and giggled. "Really?"

There were also titters from the other members in the van. The only one who didn't, was Kawa who looked round with a scowl.

"How would you know? Don't tell me you've been putting yourself about! Who have you been with?"

"That's none of your business!" Mahina spat back at her brother. "Don't tell me that you are still a virgin? I won't be able to choose who I marry, so why shouldn't I be able to choose who I have my first sex with? At least I made sure that it was someone that cared about me!"

"It's not the same for blokes, and you know it!"

Mahina shook her head at him. "As you can see, Reka. Double standards are alive and well!"

"What do you mean, that you can't choose who you marry?" Reka was astonished to hear this from Mahina, who was the most independent person she knew.

Mahina sighed. "Marriages within the tribes are usually organised by the iwi. I will be lucky if I end up with someone that likes and cares about me." Reka squeezed Mahina's hand. She fell silent as she thought of what might have been, with Kiwa.

A couple of stops for comfort and food broke the long drive. After six hours, another member took over the driving. They still had a few hours to reach their destination at Franz.


Reka took a good look out the window as they passed the pa at Arahura. Standing on the side of the road was Tui, Moana's neighbour.

As the van approached, she took a good look at it, then put her hand to her lips and blew a kiss at the van as it passed. This act broke Reka's composure and she started to sob.

Kawa saw Tui's act and Reka's reaction to it. "Who was that?" he asked sharply. He wasn't happy that someone knew they were coming.

"It's my Aunt's neighbour." Reka managed to say. "She must have told her that I had been kidnapped and was coming this way."

Tui had received a tearful call from Moana in the morning, telling of Reka's kidnapping and her probable destination. Tui had taken a chair to the roadside, getting up whenever a car or van passed to check the occupants. Seeing the van with two maori men in the front, Tui just knew that Reka and her friend were in there. An unmarked police car happened to be following them to Hokitika. The officer saw the blown kiss and the sad look on the elder maori woman's face. She knew something about that van that no-one else did!

The officer put the van's registration in his onboard computer. It came back as an Auckland plate. The missing girls were from Auckland. He was about to put his siren on to stop the van, when an emergency call came through that needed his attention. He would have to follow this up later. The officer's siren caused panic in the van, which obediently slowed to the side. There was much relief when it passed them in a hurry. However, the officer took a video of the van as he passed with his rear vision camera. He would also be investigating that later too.

It was dark when they arrived at their motel at Franz Joseph. Reka and Mahina were just glad to crash onto the bed that they shared.

They didn't care that Kawa was sharing the room with them. The sound and smell of coffee being brewed woke Reka in the morning. She could tell by the light, that it was still early. The bathroom was free, so Reka took advantage to have a much needed shower. When she put her clothes back on, she had to block out of her mind the fact that she would have to shed them altogether.

By the time the van had left Franz Joseph township, Wanaka police had been advised to look out for their van. Members of an Auckland gang were aboard and it was suspected that the two missing girls were there too. They now knew that Reka had been the target of the Kidnapping and that Mahina was unwittingly caught up in the snatch too. The fact that Mahina's brother was involved, indicated that Mahina would remain safe, but thanks to Hori's information, they knew that both Kiwa in Manapouri and Reka's lives were in danger.

The police also were aware that the gang from the pa at Arahura were also making their way through the Haast in a car. Kiwa's brother was among them. Unmarked cars were sent to follow the gangs to Wanaka, where another vehicle would take over observation of the vehicles. A car and caravan followed the van down the coast to Haast, so the van occupants didn't notice the unmarked car also following them. When the van stopped at Haast, the officer also pulled in for a break.

He returned to his car and set off before the van, confirming that he had seen the two girls. At the Gates of Haast Bridge, the officer stopped and pretended to take some photos till the van passed him, then returned to the road.

When the van approached Queenstown, Kawa turned to the girls.

"You need to say your goodbyes. We are taking Mahina and Toro to the airport first."

"You need to take us to the shops first!" Mahina countered.

"We haven't time for one of your shopping trips!" Kawa growled.

Mahina ignored her brother. "Toro, we need an overnight bag for you and a handbag for me! We will look suspicious if we rock up with no luggage at all!"

Kawa sighed. Mahina was right! "Toro, we will drop you at the shops car park. We will book in at the motel and come back for you."

Reka took a deep breath after she and Mahina had a last cuddle.

"I refuse to say goodbye." Mahina began. "Take care and stay strong."

"You too."

Mahina's gaze lingered as Reka obediently entered the motel, with Kawa and the other gang member. She didn't say a word, but she thought she saw the car that followed them through from Wanaka do a slow drive by. Hope rose within her that the car was the police. It meant there was hope that Reka would be saved after all! For the first time in her life, Mahina hoped that the police were watching.

Back at the carpark, Toro was grinning with triumph. He had a bulging overnight bag. He tossed the bag in the back with Mahina as he climbed in the front with the driver. When Mahina opened the overnight bag, she had to restrain herself from squealing with delight!

Toro had bought her a brand name handbag, in the colour she liked. Inside was a matching purse with cash. She noticed the silk negligée and mohair wrap for her and some boxers for him. She wanted to kiss him, but that would have to wait for later!

"Will it do?" Toro asked casually.

"Yeah, it will do, thanks." Mahina was just as casual.

Their check-in was uneventful and they proceeded to the gate lounge while they waited for their flight to be called. Mahina made a visit to the ladies while they were waiting. She was followed in by a female policewoman.

She introducing herself. "You are Mahina, aren't you?" Mahina nodded. "Are you okay? I can arrange for your companion to be arrested."

"There is no need, thanks. Toro is taking good care of me and will make sure that I get back to my parents."

The officer nodded. "They will be at the airport to meet you."

"I just hope," Mahina began, and she had to fight hard to keep the tears out of her eyes, "that someone will rescue Reka. They need to get to her before Te Anau. Instructions have been given to strip her and dispose of her clothes before the meeting near Manapouri. They intend to gang rape her in front of her boyfriend Kiwa and kill them..." Mahina's voice trailed off.

The policewoman took her in her arms and gave her a cuddle.

"Who are they meeting?"

"The gang from the pa at Arahura. Kiwa's brother Ben has ordered it."

"Try not to worry. We will do everything we can to keep her safe."

"Thanks."

Mahina quickly washed her face under the tap to freshen up before going out to Toro, who was beginning to be concerned at the time Mahina was taking in the ladies. She gave him a big smile and squeezed his hand when she returned.

"That's better!"

At the motel, Reka was feeling vulnerable. She was aware that now Mahina was gone, there was nothing to stop the remaining gang members from doing whatever they wanted with her. On entering the motel she checked the bathroom and the bedrooms. One had a double bed, the other had two singles. Reka returned to the living area and sat in a chair while the other gang members sat on the couch and surfed the channels on the television. She was relieved when they found some rugby to watch. It would keep their attention off her. She pretended to be interested in the match.

When the gang member returned from the airport, he and Kawa went out to fetch some dinner. After their meal they settled down to some more rugby. Reka didn't realise how tired she was and soon was sound asleep with her head on the arm of the chair. The next thing she knew, Reka was being picked up and taken into the bedroom with the twin beds. Kawa didn't comment on the fear that was showing in Reka's eyes as she was carried into the bedroom. He gently put her on the bed before turning to rejoin the others in the other room, shutting the door behind him.

Reka had no idea what time it was when she was woken, but the sky was grey and it was raining.

It felt like the sky was weeping in sympathy with her mood. Externally she was calm, but internally she was screaming at what lay ahead of her. Reka managed to shower and dress with some semblance of normality, but when it came to having breakfast, she only nibbled at it.

"I'm not hungry." Reka explained when she binned the breakfast that had been brought for her.

In the van they took their positions, with a gang member sitting next to Reka in the back. After the turnoff to Te Anau from Lumsden, Kawa turned with a stony face to make the order that she had been dreading.

"It's time to strip!" He must have seen the hint of rebellion in Reka's eyes. "If you don't, he will have much pleasure in ripping them off you!"

Reka took a deep breath and started to remove her clothes. When it came to her underwear, Reka hesitated.

"All of them!" Kawa ordered when he saw her hesitate. Reka had to slap the gang member's hand away as he reached for her bra strap and quickly removed her underwear. Without her clothes, it didn't take long for Reka to feel cold. She had a look over the back for the blanket they had been wrapped in, but it wasn't to be seen. She realised that it would have been disposed of long ago. They didn't want any evidence of the kidnapping left in the van.

"What are you looking for?" the gang member asked as he saw her looking in the back.

"Nothing. It doesn't matter." Reka muttered as she crossed her arms and legs in a vain effort to keep warm. On the road they came to a picnic area.

"Pull in here." Kawa ordered the driver. He looked at Reka who was ignoring him to look out the window.

"Pass me the clothes." Kawa ordered the gang member next to her.

Once Reka's clothes were removed from the van to the rubbish bin, the reality of her situation now hit home. Reka started to panic. It was all she could do not to start screaming. She took some deep breaths to steady herself, but it didn't make any difference. Reka couldn't help herself.

"You bastards!" Reka screamed. "You've brought me here to die! I hope you rot in Hell!"

Reka started beating the gang member next to her as she kept screaming and crying in her rage and fear. Once he grabbed her hands, a cloth with the now familiar smell of chloroform came over her mouth and nose to relieve the misery Reka was now feeling.

Now unconscious, Reka's limp form was laid on the floor at the back of the van as it continued on its way to Te Anau.

"She did well to last that long." The driver commented." By the way, we have company behind us."

In the police van behind them, the police woman lowered the binoculars she was holding.

"We need to rescue Reka now! She's been stripped and is unconscious!"

# CONFRONTATION

Finding Kiwa was a much harder task for the gang at Invercargill. They went from town to town, looking for evidence of him. The gang had the model, colour and registration plate of Kiwa's car, but there was no sign of it.

It wasn't untill the gang came to Manapouri nearly six months later, that they saw a car in the camping ground with a cover over it, which immediately raised their suspicions. They took a trip to the supermarket while waiting for night to fall. A casual look at the community notice board while they were filling in time, showed them, in bold letters, an advert from Kiwa advertising his services. A quick check after dark, confirmed that the car was his. They now had Kiwa's location. The gang booked themselves into the camping ground for a week to keep an eye on Kiwa's routine. When they contacted Ben, they were told to just observe Kiwa till they arrived.

When Kiwa saw the gang from Invercargill move into the chalet opposite him, he knew his quiet life here was over. He now needed to move on, but to where? Kiwa found on the first day of their stay, that whenever he left the camp, someone followed him to observe everything he did. This meant that his routine of attending martial arts had to cease. He didn't want the gang to know that he had the ability to defend himself.

The true reason the Invercargill gang were here, became apparent when Kiwa received the call from Hori that Reka had been kidnapped. He knew immediately that Reka was being brought here!

Kiwa realised that not only his time here was over, but his life was over as well. Kiwa tried to work out how long he had before the Arahura pa gang arrived. There was no point now, in keeping his car covered, so Kiwa went out to uncover it.

"Going somewhere mate?" one of the gang called out from the chalet balcony.

"I'm not your mate and its none of your F...... business! You mongrels!"

"Who are you calling a Mongrel?" The gang member sprang up from his seat.

"I'm calling you all Mongrels!" Kiwa shouted at him. "I know you are here to make sure I die!"

With that Kiwa turned on his heel and slammed his door behind him. Kiwa had jobs to do. He might as well do them while he still could. It would keep his mind off what was coming. There was a knock at the door.

"Who is it?" Kiwa growled. He wasn't in any mood to be social.

"I want to talk." Kiwa looked out the window. It was one of the gang.

"There isn't anything to talk about. Get off my porch!"

"How do you know?"

"My girlfriend's father told me that she's been kidnapped. I know she is being brought here to be abused and to watch me die. Now f... off! If any of you come near me, I will make sure you die as well!"

Kiwa sat on a chair and closed his eyes to meditate, till he calmed himself. He knew he was being watched through the window, but he didn't care. It wasn't untill the footsteps moved off the porch, and crossed to their chalet, that Kiwa made the move to leave. He ignored the gang sitting on the porch opposite.

As Kiwa moved around the town, doing the jobs that had been booked, the gang were there too, but they were keeping a respectful distance. Kiwa was mowing a lawn when a toot made him look up. It was Daniel, the leader at the Martial arts classes. He shouted out.

"Where were you last night? We missed you!"

Kiwa pointed at the gang who were watching him. He also indicated that he would give Daniel a call. Daniel took one look at the occupants, gave Kiwa the thumbs up and left. Between jobs, Kiwa called Daniel and explained his situation.

"Just remember, you're not alone and have friends here." Daniel told him. Daniel was already looking at ways Kiwa could be protected.

During the remainder of the day, Kiwa's mates from the martial arts club came driving past where Kiwa was working. The gang soon found that they were being scrutinised as well. When Kiwa returned to his chalet, he found that Daniel was following him and parked his car next to Kiwa's.

"From now on, one of us will be with you at all times." Daniel told Kiwa after he let him in the chalet. "How long have we got before they get here? and how many can we expect."

"They could come either tomorrow or the day after. My brother's gang will have five at least. I don't know how many are coming with Reka. I would say at least another three. That's not counting these goons as well." Kiwa indicated the gang opposite.

"Have you got any work on tomorrow?"

"No. I've cleared the decks. I might seem calm, but I'm not feeling it. I don't think I could do any, anyway." As they were talking, Kiwa thought he heard someone come on the balcony.

"Get off my balcony!" Kiwa shouted furiously as he came to the window. The local police officer was at the door. Kiwa immediately opened the door and motioned him to come in.

"Sorry." Kiwa apologised. "I thought you were the gang across from me come to harass me. You should keep an eye through the window to make sure they don't try to sneak over to listen in.

"Are they armed?" the sergeant wanted to know.

"They haven't displayed any. That doesn't mean they don't have some."

"Hello Daniel. What brings you here?" the sergeant wanted to know. He knew of Daniel's martial arts training classes.

"We've started a roster to protect him."

"So, it's true then, that your life is in danger."

Kiwa nodded. "I know they will kill me." Saying it with a flat finality that couldn't be ignored. His eyes held a bleak acceptance of something he couldn't hide from.

"I've heard that one lot are at Haast and the others are at Franz Joseph."

"My brother Ben's gang will be at Haast. They will probably try to grab me when they get here tomorrow."

"How many of them are there? and will they be armed?"

"There will be at least five in Ben's gang coming. My brother has a pistol. The others have the usual - knives, knuckledusters, and chains."

"So that's a yes for weapons." The sergeant made a note in his pad.

"Of course we have these lot from Invercargill keeping tabs on me till they get here." Kiwa added.

"Are they now!  What about the gang at Franz Joseph?"

"There will be at least three of them.  They kidnapped my girlfriend Reka and are bringing her to Ben.  Ben's gang intend to gang rape her in front of me before they kill me."

"It's good you have someone with you.  I will be keeping an eye on you as well."

"Thanks."

The officer went outside and strode to the chalet opposite, where the gang were all out on the balcony, trying to catch what was being said in Kiwa's chalet.

"You lot be packed up and be ready to leave town in half an hour.  If you don't leave, or show up here again, you will be enjoying the hospitality of my cells!"

There was some relief when the chalet opposite became quiet and silent, with the departure of the gang.  After the sergeant left the camp ground, he rang Invercargill.

"I've got trouble coming tomorrow.  I need at least at least three armed officers to man road blocks coming into town."

"I can only give you Bruce.  He's a senior constable.  You will have to manage the best you can."

Phone calls were made to a couple of local deerstalkers, Phil and Dave, to enlist their help.

When Bruce arrived, He was sent with Dave to the Hillside Manapouri Road, while the sergeant and Phil took the main road in from Te Anau.

Daniel stayed with Kiwa for the night, which helped him to get some rest. When Garry came to relieve Daniel was in the morning, Daniel gave Kiwa's shoulder a squeeze.

"Get some pizzas and beer in for tonight! We all will be here to support you!"

"Shouldn't we be taking Kiwa somewhere else, if the gang are coming here and let the cops be here to meet them?" Garry asked.

"It's a good point. I will ask the sergeant."

"Thanks." Kiwa showed his gratitude. "I will get the pizzas and beer in anyway."

When Ben rang the Invercargill gang for an update the next morning, they didn't answer his call, but sent a text.

"You're on your own. The cops kicked us out of town".

Ben realised then, that his plans would have to change. He couldn't rock up to the camp ground as a guest of the Invercargill gang. They would have to sneak in during the night and snatch Kiwa. He had a look at google maps. They would have to change the route into Manapouri and arrange a new meeting place. He tried ringing Kawa, but he didn't answer either; so he texted him.

"Meet before Te Anau."

"Okay." The answering text came back.

When Ben and his gang came through the pass to Wanaka and Queenstown, they were aware of police cars parked at various points. The gang were relieved that none of them tried to pull them over. After a break in Queenstown, they pressed on. It was nearly dark, when they came across a sign "Hillside Manapouri Road".

"We turn here." Ben advised Luke, who was driving. Luke obeyed.

"We aren't going through Te Anau?"

"No. It's quicker and the cops won't be expecting us to come this way."

They were surprised to find a solitary police officer stop them on the edge of town. As Bruce reached Luke's open window, Ben reached across Luke and shot him at almost point blank range in the high abdomen. Bruce found himself flat on his back on the ground as the car sped off. Dave was hiding behind Bruce's police car, took aim with his rifle and shot at the back tyre, but missed. He then aimed for the back window. He was pleased to see the middle head in the back seat slump. He then ran over to Bruce, who was getting his breath back

"Just as well I was wearing my vest! We had better get after them!"

In Ben's car there was grim determination as Dillon's body slumped in the back seat. They hadn't expected to lose anyone on this trip! The sergeant and Phil heard the shots in the distance and immediately headed back into town.

At the motor camp, Daniel and Kiwa's mates from the club had gathered in his chalet, bringing their sleeping bags with them. They had finished their pizzas and were relaxing with a quiet beer. The sergeant had reassured them that he intended to prevent Ben's gang from reaching the township.

The sound of pistol and rifle shots nearby put Kiwa on full alert. Mike was nearest to the light.

"Mike! Turn the light off!" Kiwa said as he put his beer down. "It sounds like Ben's gang is here!"

Mike hastened to obey as everyone else immediately went on guard. All was quiet until Daniel thought he heard a noise in the bathroom. In the dim light he could see a figure climbing in the window. A swift hard karate chop sent the intruder into a slump.

A second one broke his neck.  Daniel pushed the body back out onto the ground.  Daniel was going to shut the window, when two shots whizzed past his ear!  He ducked down low to the side of the window in case the gunman came in that way.

In the main living room there was commotion as other members of the gang burst in the door.  One tried to find the light, only to find his arm being twisted into a position that his body had to follow.  He found himself on the floor screaming in pain till he was silenced.

Kiwa waited in the bedroom, next to the window, when a blow with a pistol butt broke it, sending glass showering over him.  Kiwa's brother Ben put a leg over the sill, peering into the room.  As Ben swept the room with his gun, Kiwa knocked the gun out of his hand, sending it flying across the room.  As the gun hit the leg of the bed, it went off.  The bullet hit Kiwa in the ankle, but as he was grappling with Ben, he didn't notice till later, when someone asked about the blood on his ankle.

Ben was bigger than Kiwa, but Kiwa was now much fitter and stronger, than him.  So when Ben tried to strangle him, Kiwa had no trouble in dislodging Ben's hands and used a judo throw to send him flying onto the bed.

"Move left Kiwa!" Dave's voice ordered him.

As soon as Kiwa complied with the order, two rifle shots rang out to render Ben lifeless.

As the sergeant was approaching the camp entrance, he received a call from the camp manager.

"How quick can you get here? There's a fight going on in Kiwa's chalet!  It sounds like shots are being fired!

"We heard the shots. We are about to arrive."

171

In the chalet, the surviving gang member was being held by Mike in a headlock. When he saw Kiwa he vented his fury.

"You've managed to kill everyone else, but you just wait! I won't rest till I've killed you both! Even if it takes my whole life to do it! I'll have my revenge!"

Mike didn't say a word, but in a single action snapped his neck- just as the sergeant came to the door.

"I hope you had a good reason for doing that!" The sergeant said to Mike. He had a look at the bodies and the damage around the place. "I will be wanting statements from you all in the morning. In the meantime nothing is to be touched. We will need forensics from Invercargill to come. Bruce the constable and Dave came in behind him. Bruce was carrying the rifle. The sergeant noticed a bullet lodged in Bruce's vest.

"You took one as well!"

Bruce nodded. "It was at the traffic stop out of town. I wouldn't be here without it."

"Has anyone got any injuries?" the sergeant wanted to know. They all looked each other over. It was then that the bullet wound to Kiwa's ankle was found. A call came in from the clinic nurse, who like everyone else in town, had heard the shooting.

"Am I needed at all?"

"A bullet wound to the ankle."

"Get someone to bring them over."

"Bruce come with me. I have a spare bed for visitors."

"You will be seeing the manager?" Kiwa asked. The sergeant nodded. "Tell him I'm sorry about the damage. I will fix it once forensics have finished."

At the clinic, the nurse checked Kiwa's wound. He winced as she probed and located the bullet.

"I should be sending you off to the hospital for an op. Will you be okay if I put in some local anaesthetic to remove the bullet, clean the wound and pop in a couple of stitches?"

"Go for it."

Afterwards, everyone retired to Daniel's house. A medicinal beer was enjoyed by all. Kiwa appreciated a pillow and some blankets to rest on Daniel's couch for the remainder of the night, though his thoughts kept turning to Reka. He was relieved that the danger from Ben's gang was now gone. He just hoped Reka wasn't being abused by the gang who were bringing her.

It was early in the morning when Daniel came out to the kitchen.

"Can't you sleep either Daniel?" Kiwa asked.

"No." Daniel sighed. I'm pretty sure the sergeant will try to charge us and maybe kick us out of town. I could see he wasn't happy when he saw Mike break the neck of that bloke that was threatening you. Post mortems will show that three of them had their necks broken."

"I fully expect that to happen for me," Kiwa began "but why would he do that to you? You were only acting to protect me!"

"Yeah, but once we become proficient in Martial arts, our bodies are considered weapons. Once you get your belts, you will have to register with the cops too. If they consider we have overstepped the use of our "weapon" we can be charged. I won't be able to teach if that happens."

"Will you be coming with me then, when I leave?" Kiwa asked.

"Probably. Where do you think you will go?

"Now that my brother's gang is gone, it will be safest for me to go to the West Coast where I come from."

"I don't suppose you have any lakes like this one over there?"

Kiwa grinned at him. "We have quite a few for you to pick from."

When the sergeant knocked the door at breakfast time, both Daniel and Kiwa were showered and dressed and had their statements ready for him.

"Kiwa, the forensic team are here. Once they have finished, you will have half an hour to pack and leave town." Kiwa nodded his agreement.

"Daniel, I want a word with you too!" the sergeant began.

"Thanks for putting me up for the night, Daniel." Kiwa interrupted him. "I will head back to the camp now."

"Call me before you leave." Daniel told him as Kiwa departed.

"I will do." Kiwi replied.

Kiwa started to walk back to the camp. He was slower than usual as the wound in his foot was making its presence felt. Back at the camp, Kiwa met with the manager.

"I'm sorry about everything that happened." Kiwa began. "I did tell the sergeant that I would fix everything up after forensics left, but he advised me this morning he wants me out of town half an hour after they finish. How much do you think it will cost to clean and fix up the chalet?"

"A grand."

Kiwa give him his savings account card. "Take it out of this."

For the first time, the manager smiled. "I wish you well."

Kiwa was sitting in his car, as he waited for the team to finish in the chalet, when a call came on his phone. It was Hori, asking if he was okay.

"I am - apart from a little bullet hole in my ankle. Is there any word on Reka?"

"Yes." There was relief in Hori's voice. "She's been rescued and is being taken to the hospital in Queenstown. We are flying down there on the next flight."

"I will see you there. I'm coming back to the coast to live."

The sound of the police siren made the van driver pull up. The gang were hoping that it would pass them for another job, but their luck was out this time. The police van pulled in behind them. Another police car came from behind to park in front of the van. Officers jumped out with rifles trained on Kawa and the driver.

"It's over." Kawa said flatly as he put his hands up. The driver did the same.

The van doors opened at the back.

"Why is she naked? and what have you given Reka for her to be in this state?" The police woman yelled at them, as she covered Reka with a blanket. She could see Reka was shivering, a sign she was going into hypothermia. The police woman turned to the officer with her. "We need a helicopter to get her to hospital." The officer quickly ran back to the police van to radio her request.

Kawa turned round to face the police woman.

"She's naked because we were ordered to deliver her that way. Reka was fine untill we took her clothes away, then she went berserk. The only way we could calm her was to give her some chloroform."

"Have you had sex with her?"

"We haven't touched her."

"Who were you delivering her to?" Kawa remained silent.

"It wasn't Ben and his gang from the coast, by any chance?"

"What about them?"

"They are all dead."

The door beside Kawa opened. "Have you any weapons on you or in the van?"

"No."

Kawa knew that they wouldn't be going home now, for quite some time. – years in fact.

As Reka regained awareness, she realised she was in a bed, and it was warm! Someone was holding her hand and giving it a squeeze. Reka squeezed it back.

"She's awake at last!" Kohi's voice spoke. "Reka love! We are here!"

Reka opened her eyes. Both her mother and father were here! She gave them a smile. Then Reka remembered being forced to be naked and given chloroform. The horror of her ordeal showed in her face.

"Did they....? Why aren't I dead? What happened to Kiwa?"

"No they didn't." Kohi reassured Reka. There was a fight at Manapouri, but Kiwa's friends and the police stopped Ben's gang from harming him. He has a bullet wound in the ankle, but is otherwise fine. The gang is dead, so you won't have to worry about them anymore. Kiwa is coming to see you too. He said he is coming back to the Coast to live."

Reka's nurse bustled in to take some observations. She was happy to see Reka was awake and that her observations were now back to normal. Her doctor came shortly afterwards, and after asking how Reka was feeling, advised that she would be discharged tomorrow.

While Hori and Kohi visited the café, Reka had a little doze. She felt a hand grab hold of hers. A familiar tingle went through her fingers!

Reka's eyes shot open. Kiwa was here and he was bending over her! Her love for him was shining in her eyes as she used her other hand to bring his head down for the kiss they had been denied for so long.

When the family left for the coast the next morning, behind Kiwa's car, there was a small convoy. Daniel, Mike and Garry were also coming with them. Mike was towing a large caravan and Garry was towing his boat. They had been allowed to leave Manapouri with no charges against them, after giving a signed undertaking that they would never use their bodies as a weapon to kill ever again.

By the time the family had reached their home at Kaniere Road, Reka was mentally much improved from her ordeal. Moana had been given Hoani's old room and had made herself comfortable in there. She had no desire to return to the pa, but missed Tui, so they now had a weekly lunch at the café in town.

Reka enjoyed a night of comfort in her own room before catching the plane back to Auckland. Reka needed to finish her training course, before she returned home. She intended to set up a child care centre when her course was completed. Saying goodbye to Kiwa was difficult, but they both knew that this time it was only temporary. They could look forward to a future together.

When Reka was reunited with Mahina, they had a big cuddle. Mahina had prepared herself for the fact that she wouldn't see her friend again, so they had plenty to talk about the events since.

"I was a very naughty girl on the plane!" Mahina told Reka. "You may remember I spoke about losing my virginity?"

"How could I forget!" Reka laughed. "What happened?"

"You know Toro took me home. Well, he was the one I chose. He made it clear that he still cares and he wants to marry me. He has even spoke to the iwi!" Mahina took a big breath and became more serious as she continued. "I knew we wouldn't be together for a long while after we got home, so I took him to the bathroom with me!"

At Reka's gasp of amazement and mirth, Mahina nodded.

"I don't regret it. The police were waiting for him as soon as we arrived in the terminal. Luckily I had already said my goodbyes before we got off the plane." Mahina's eyes looked bleak as she continued. "He is looking at a couple of years inside for his involvement in the kidnapping, though he may be out sooner for good behaviour." Mahina put a protective hand over her stomach, which Reka picked up on straight away.

"You aren't pregnant by any chance?"

"I think I may be, but it is too early to tell yet. At least this course will be finished by then."

"What will your parents say?"

"They won't be happy, that's for sure."

"Well, one thing is for sure," and Reka took Mahina's hand in her's. "You aren't doing this alone!"

Mike had been invited to bring his caravan to the Kaniere Road property, where he, Daniel, Garry and Kiwa slept while they were establishing themselves. One weekend they all went out to the bach at Lake Kaniere with the family. Mike went for a walk with Hoani around the bush blocks nearby where was one for sale.

On the Monday Mike put an offer on it, which was accepted. Hori and Hoani helped him to clear an area big enough for the caravan and a pole framed home, which gave Mike plenty of storage underneath and views of the lake up on the living area; which became a favourite place for them to catch up on weekends when they weren't out fishing on one of the West Coast lakes.

Both Mike and Garry found jobs helping on farms over in the Kokatahi and Kowhitirangi area. They became very popular with farmers, giving them a much needed break from the arduous twice daily task of milking their herds when the farmers wanted a holiday. They also met their wives during their working days in the district.

Daniel found a home he liked, on the hill overlooking Greymouth. He made a visit to the local police station to register. They had heard about the incident in Manapouri and were interested to hear all the details. When the police saw that it was a one-off incident that wouldn't be happening again, they were happy for Daniel to set up a martial arts academy in Greymouth. Some of the younger officers also joined in the classes, including a woman pc Cheryl who insisted on some "private tuition". Senior staff at the station were happy they had an "insider" involved at the academy and encouraged the relationship. In time Cheryl helped Daniel to run classes for children.

Kiwa still loved the sea, and after hearing of the fishing fleet based at Greymouth, found a job on one of the vessels. After advising the skipper he had previous experience, Kiwa was mortified on his first trip out to be spending half the time with his head over the side, much to the mirth of his mates.

However, the skipper could see the way Kiwa handled himself and the equipment, that he knew his way around a boat, and was happy to keep him on.

One morning after the trawler returned to dock, Kiwa took a back street as a short cut on the way south, and passed an old house that was for sale. There was permission to rebuild, but Kiwa knew this grand old lady was waiting for someone to come to restore her. A visit to the real estate for a price and a tour convinced Kiwa this would be his and Reka's new home. He took some photos and sent them to Reka.

"These are "Before" photos of our new home. What do you think?"

"I think it is wonderful!"

Reka had trouble concentrating on her lessons the next day. Her mind kept wandering to the home that was waiting for her at Greymouth.

Once the sale was completed, much of Kiwa's spare time was now spent on restoring the home to its glory; with input from Reka on the colour scheme and also the appliances and furnishings in the house.

During their remaining time in Auckland, Reka and Mahina also learnt to drive. They both knew they would need their driving licences in their new lives. When Reka drove home six months later, she had Mahina with her. Mahina was now visibly pregnant. She had been encouraged to adopt her baby out, but Mahina was determined to keep her baby, even if it meant bringing it up alone. Mahina had a large suitcase full of baby clothes, a fold down pram and a carry basket packed in the back along with her own luggage. Kiwa had been happy to have Mahina come to live with them while she needed support.

Kiwa was mindful of the support that he also needed in the final days he spent at Manapouri.

Hori had given Reka instructions to come to their home first, when they returned. Reka was pleased to see the gates were back open as she turned in the drive.

"Oh!" Reka exclaimed when she saw not only the family cars, but also other familiar cars were here. Also the men were around a hangi in the paddock!

"What's wrong?" Mahina looked concerned .

"Nothing's wrong!" Reka turned to Mahina with a grin. "Kiwa is formally being welcomed into our family and to become my husband tonight!"

"How do you know? Didn't they tell you?" Mahina was shocked that this was being sprung on Reka.

"They didn't tell me, but they did something similar for my brother Hoani and his wife Lucy when she came home from her studies. I know it is happening, as the local iwi's cars are here, and a hangi has been put down!" Reka looked at Mahina. "You will be able to help me prepare for my civil wedding!"

As Reka parked the hire car, Kiwa came running over.

"I've got something to tell you!" Kiwa began.

"I already know!" Reka grinned at him. "I saw the iwi's cars!"

"Not only that, but my parents are here! They have come to terms with the fact that I have chosen my own path in life, which is a successful one. We have reconciled and they would also like to welcome you to our family."

"I'm glad that has happened for you!" Reka began, "and if you think it is okay, I will be happy to join your family."

The relief on Kiwa's face told her of his nervousness of how she would react.  Reka put her hand in his.

"It will be fine.  Like all new relationships, it will take time to adjust to them and them to us."

Kiwa's reaction was to reach in and give her a big kiss.

"There's plenty of time for that later!"  Kohi's voice interrupted them.  "Come inside Mahina and Reka!  We have to get you ready!"

Kohi gave Kiwa a playful push out of the way as she opened the car door to help her daughter out and gave her a big hug before taking the girls indoors. Moana, Amy and Lucy were also there to welcome them. Behind them a lady with features similar to Kiwa's was also waiting.  Reka gave her an encouraging smile.

"You are Rangi? Welcome to the family!"  Reka put out her hand.  Rangi took her hand and drew Reka to her to put their heads together.

"Welcome to our family too!"  Reka could see sadness in Rangi's eyes.

"I see you are still healing.  I am sorry for your loss." Reka said simply.

"How can you say that, after what he tried to do to you? I wouldn't be so forgiving!"

"I'm not a parent yet, but my parents love us and support us, even if they don't agree with us.  I'm sure you do the same."

Rangi turned to Kohi. "You have raised her well."

Kohi smiled and took Reka to her room.  The two single beds had been replaced by a double bed.   On the bed lay a traditional dress and cloak for Reka to wear. She could hear Hori and Kiwa in her parents room and knew he too was being "dressed"

They waited for Hori and Kiwa to leave before they joined the ladies in the kitchen.

When the Karanga call came, Kohi and Rangi together led Reka followed by Moana, Mahina, Amy and Lucy out to the new house. Emily and Alice also followed the ladies. Alice was holding a woven bag in her hands. Kiwa's father, Kapia and Hori led Kiwa, with Terry, Hoani and Jimmy following behind them. Jimmy was also carrying a woven bag.

The ground floor had been decorated in traditional symbols and tree ferns with a long table set up for the feast. After Kiwa and Reka were joined together for their pledge, Jimmy and Alice came forward with the bags they had been carrying to the iwi. Inside the bag Alice carried, was a Pounamu taonga shaped in a fish hook, which was given from Hori's family to Kiwa. Inside the bag that Jimmy carried was the pounamu taonga of the bird which was given from Kapia's family to Reka.

When Reka and Kiwa finally were alone together, they revelled in the freedom to express their love for each other, that they had to contain for so long.

The next day, they said their goodbyes to the family, promising to see them again soon. When Kiwa took his parents back to the pa, all of his and Reka's gear was now in his car. When Mahina and Reka drove the hire car back to the car depot, they also had a stop at the car yards on the way; to check for cars available in their price range. Mahina and Reka had pooled their remaining money, given to them while in training and found they had enough for a second hand car, which would give them independence when Kiwa was working.

When Reka and Mahina finally arrived at the depot where Kiwa was waiting for them, he looked pointedly at his watch with a quizzical smile.

"I thought you had got lost!"

"We think we have found our car!" Reka replied.

"You will have to show it to me!" Kiwa grinned, wondering what they had found. When he saw it, Kiwa was pleasantly surprised, that their "find" was a little gem! In good condition and low mileage too, at a reasonable price. "I can get this for you."

The girls gasped. "We don't expect you to do this!"

"I know, but you want to start up a child care centre, aren't you? Well, that is going to cost you money to set up."

They saw the wisdom of Kiwa's words and accepted his offer to pay for their car.

At their new home, Reka loved the space in the house that she had only seen in photos. In the back yard, there was a large shed that had been a "man cave" with facilities already installed, that could easily be converted into a suitable place to care for children. In the coming weeks, both Reka and Mahina were busy with transforming the shed into a suitable place for children to be cared for. The back yard also received attention, with suitable secure fencing and safe play equipment with cover over it for any changes in weather. Most important of all, the girls compiled the manuals and documentation that they needed for their business.

When the neighbours saw and heard what they were doing, word soon spread and before long there were parents knocking the door wanting to know when their centre was opening.

When the girls contacted the council to obtain a permit, and were given a checklist of requirement;, they only had to obtain written approval from their neighbours before they submitted it. There were celebrations the day the approval came through and were able to contact all the people who had put their name on the waiting list.

By the time Mahina's baby was due, the day care centre was running well for the girls, giving them a good income, which Kiwa appreciated as well. It took the pressure off him to work at sea. Although Kiwa loved his work, there had been a couple of trips in dangerous seas that had him reconsidering his work there.

# MAHINA AND TORO'S NEW FAMILY

As she watched Reka and Kiwa's ceremony, Mahina wondered with envy whether she would enjoy a ceremony to make her pledge and welcome to family as Reka and Kiwa had done. She would have to have a talk to Toro about it! After the blessing of the Pounamu Taonga and the couple by the iwi, they sat down for their hangi. Mahina found herself sitting between Moana and Rangi at the table.

"Moana, can you tell Tui, that both Reka and I want to thank her for being there, when the van went past. It helped us to know that someone knew what was happening us and cared."

Moana took Mahina's hand and gave it a squeeze.

"It was a hard time for us all!"

Both Moana and Rangi were interested to hear how she was enjoying her pregnancy and had any names been picked yet.

"I have to admit, I haven't had time to even think about babies names yet." Mahina told them. "After Reka and I were returned from our little adventure in the van, we had some catching up to do with our studies and also we knew we would need our drivers licences as well when we finished. I have had little time to think of myself till now, except for monthly visits to check the baby is progressing well. My next priority is to help Reka set up our child care centre. I need an income sorted for when the baby is born."

"The father isn't around?" Rangi asked.

Mahina gave her a wry smile. "He is serving time for his part in our kidnapping!"

"No!" Rangi showed her shock. "You weren't raped by him?!"

Mahina was able to smile. "No. I knew Toro before we were kidnapped. They had no idea that they had kidnapped me with Reka untill it was too late. I hope to marry Toro some day."

"What about your family?" Moana asked. "Don't they approve?"

Mahina's heart sank as she faced reality. "I don't think they do." Mahina's eyes were sad as she looked at the happy faces of Reka and Kiwa across the table. "Mum wanted me to have the baby adopted out. I'm determined that isn't going to happen, even if I have to bring it up by myself."

"That's a long hard road for you if it happens that way." Rangi commented.

Mahina nodded her agreement. "I hope it doesn't, but I'm prepared for it."

In the prison, Toro had just got his phone back. He tried to phone Mahina, but it went straight to message bank, so he texted her instead.

"Good news! If I keep my nose clean, I will be out in 3 months! Will you marry me?"

It wasn't till much later, when Mahina was retiring to the bedroom she was sharing with Moana for the night, that she thought to check her phone calls and messages. Mahina's squeal startled Moana, but the radiant look on her face told Mahina it was good news. When Mahina showed Moana the message, her beam matched Mahina's.

Toro was dozing when a flurry of messages flooded his phone.

"OMG!"

"YES! YES! YES!"

"I've just been at Reka and Kiwa's blessing and welcome to family. It was really beautiful! Can we have one?"

Toro's cellmate was disturbed by the dings from Toro's phone.

"What's up mate?"

Toro grinned. "My girl's just got the message that I want to get married."

Then another message came through.

"I have news for you too! Our little Toro is due then!Xx"

Toro's gasp had his cellmate sit up.

"I'm having a sprog!"

"Really?" His cellmate laughed. "You will have to stay on the straight and narrow now! Kids do change you!"

"If that is true, how come you're in here again?"

At that they both laughed, which drew calls from cells around them "Hey! Share the joke!" Toro texted back to Mahina.

"When is it due?"

When she gave Toro the date, he realised it was the day after he was due out.

"I will try to be there. What hospital will you be at?"

"Greymouth."

"What are you doing down there?"

"Reka and Kiwa are helping me till I get on my feet. Mum wanted me to have bub adopted! – not happening!"

"Tell them thanks! Xx"

189

When Toro ended the conversation, his cellmate, who was now sitting beside him watching the screen, made the comment.

"No sleep for you tonight."

He was right. Toro's mind was reeling with everything that he wanted and needed to be done for his family. He tried not to think of the gang responsibilities that would be expected of him too, once he was out. Toro realised then, that he had to choose one or the other. For other gang members, their families came a poor second in their lives, which the gang members accepted. For Toro, his life with Mahina was going to come first, but it was going to come at a price!

"Don't tell anyone yet!" Toro told his cellmate.

"Why?" His cellmate was puzzled Toro didn't want to share his good news.

"There are things I have to do, before it becomes public!"

"Okay." His cellmate knew immediately that Toro planned to put his family before his mates in the gang, who would make life difficult for him if they could. For Toro to have any chance of successfully making a new start, he would have to organise his affairs before anyone knew of his intentions.

A month after the proposal, Mahina came to the phone with a marriage celebrant, who would carry out the ceremony via video phone call. Reka and Kiwa witnessed the ceremony her end. Toro's cellmate and a guard witnessed it his end. Toro had been determined that his son would have his name when he was born.

Once Toro told Kawa of his intention to leave the gang, he and other gang members had a meeting with Toro.

"Why are you leaving?" Kawa asked. "Who are you joining?"

"I'm not joining anyone. I'm choosing to put Mahina first in my life."

"Did Kiwa put you up to this?"

"No. I haven't spoken to him."

While Kawa respected Toro's decision to put his sister first in his life, he couldn't let him just walk away without a severe penalty.

"You and your family will never be part of our family. I will be advising the iwi." Toro nodded his acceptance. "There is also the small matter of the account we gave you." Toro immediately handed over the bankcard and the password.

"It hasn't been touched since I made my decision."

"Good. We expect you to pay back all money you used in the account, with interest." With that, Kawa led his gang members away to the area they reserved for themselves.

The day Toro was released, his father came to collect him to take him to the airport. He was surprised to find not only his mother was there, but also Mahina's parents were there too.

"We are coming to see the new grandson." His father explained.

"Does Mahina know you're coming?"

"Not yet!" Mahina's mother piped up. "Though I don't think she will mind! We have organised ourselves a stay at the nearby hotel."

"Are you two going to just shack up?" Mahina's father wanted to know.

"We've already had the civil ceremony with a celebrant, a couple of months ago."

There was stunned silence for a few seconds before an indignant chorus. "You didn't tell anyone! Why didn't you tell us?"

"Sorry," Toro was repentant. "I was busy trying to make sure I had some money behind me when I came out," Toro paused. "I'm also out of the gang too. It's the only way that I can put Mahina first in my life."

There was another silence before Mahina's father asked. "What did Kawa say?"

"He said we would never be part of the family, and he was advising the iwi."

"Kawa doesn't have the authority to dictate who will or will not be part of our family!" Mahina's father's tone was firm.

"Seeing you missed out on the civil ceremony, perhaps we can organise a traditional pledge and welcome to the family while you are down with us?" Toro suggested. "I know Mahina wants one."

"That will be perfect!" There were beams on the faces of both the mothers.

Before they boarded the plane, Toro's phone rang. It was Mahina.

"Are you out yet?" Her voice seemed strained.

"I'm about to board the plane. Are you okay?"

"Kiwa will meet you at Hokitika Airport." There was a small pause. "I'm in labour!"

"You keep your legs crossed till I get there!"

Mahina giggled. "I'm not making any promises!" before ringing off.

"She's in labour, isn't she?" Mahina's mother asked.

"She is! Reka will be with her till we get there."

Kiwa was surprised to see both Toro and Mahina's parents had come, and was pleased that they had already organised a hire car for themselves, as they all wouldn't fit in the one car.  Kiwa and Toro had time for a good chat on the journey up to Greymouth.  When Kiwa heard that Toro was here to stay, he asked if he was interested in a job on the fishing boats.

"Thanks, but I will try to get a shore job first.  I tend to get seasick when on a boat for any length of time."

"I don't blame you! The pay is great, but I'm beginning to wonder if it is worth it.  The girls are doing really well financially, with the child care centre they have set up, so it takes the pressure off us!  I'm looking at going back to a shore job too."

At the hospital, Toro was directed to the delivery suite by the receptionist.  There he found Mahina on the bed with a glow of achievement on her face, as she looked at the bundle in Reka's arms.  Toro took Mahina in his arms to give her a kiss and a long cuddle.

"Are you okay?" Toro asked.

"I am, now you are here!"

"Are you going to meet your son?" Reka asked as she stood up for Toro to sit down in her chair.  She let herself out of the room to give them time alone together. Gingerly Toro took the bundle in his arms as Reka instructed him and looked down at the tiny face in the swaddling blankets.  Toro could see his own features in the baby's face and wondered whose eyes he had.

"He's got your eyes." Mahina said, reading Toro's thoughts.

"Have you thought of a name for him?" Toro asked, as a wave of protective love came over him.

"I have a list of names we can go through."

"Let's do it now, before the others come in!"

"Who else is coming?" Mahina wanted to know.

"It's a surprise!" Toro gave her a big grin. "They gave me a surprise as well! Where's that list?"

By the time Toro went out to fetch their parents, their son was named Tama Taiko. "He will probably get Tama, but that's okay."

Mahina's face was a picture of astonishment when Toro brought both parents in to see them. It was only when Tama starting fussing for a feed, that the parents took their leave, promising to return the following day. Mahina rang the bell for the nurse, who came in to help her to establish Tama's first feed. Seeing how vigorously his son was sucking, delighted Toro. Once Tama was settled, Toro sat and held Mahina's hand. Her eyes closed as tiredness overwhelmed her.

"I will see you tomorrow, love." Toro told Mahina as he gave her a kiss goodbye. She briefly opened her eyes to smile, before returning to sleep.

Back at Kiwa and Reka's home, Reka had dinner ready when Kiwa brought Toro and the parents back. They were all impressed at the lovely old house and the good condition it was in.

"You should have seen the state of it when I bought it!" Kiwa said, showing them the "before" photos of the house.

"It must have cost you quite a bit to get it done?" Toro asked.

"Only the materials to fix it. I did it myself."

"Where did you learn the skills to do it up? Toro wanted to know.

"When I was down south, I set up a little business doing people's gardens and odd jobs, like painting and repairing things.  I really enjoyed it, as I was doing something different every day and could choose my hours when I worked.  By the time I had finished, with my time on the boats and the handyman job, I had enough to buy this house."

"Do you reckon there is an outlet for us to do something like that here?" Toro asked.

"We should do well here." Kiwa replied.  "Most people have lawns and gardens here.  There are a lot more people in Greymouth, than at Manapouri where I was."

When Toro went to bed that night, he had plenty to think about. He needed some wheels and somewhere for him and his family to live.  Toro was grateful for Reka and Kiwa having Mahina and now him stay with them, but he wanted his own place as soon as he could.

Toro had showered and was having breakfast with Reka when Kiwa came home from his night at sea. He had a covered trailer with him.

"Well that's the last of those I'm doing!" Kiwa announced to them. "We nearly ended up down in the locker!"

Reka immediately ran over to cuddle him.  She could see by the look in Kiwa's eyes that he had looked death in the face.

"Have a few days off, before you do anything else!" Reka ordered him. Kiwa was quite happy to comply. "Whose trailer have you brought home?" Reka wanted to know when she saw it parked with his vehicle.

"It's mine." Kiwa managed to say. He didn't want to admit it, but he was feeling unwell.

When Reka raised her eyebrows, Kiwa added; "I just bought it from one of my mates on the fishing boat. He doesn't need it anymore. I'm going back to doing my gardening handyman job that I used to do."

"What about you, Toro? Have you any idea what you want to do?"

"I'm going to help Kiwa with his job."

"Are you going to have some sleep?" Reka asked Kiwa. "You look washed out!"

"Not yet!" Kiwa was looking troubled. "Every time I close my eyes, I can see myself underwater and feel like I'm drowning again!"

"If you feel like your drowning, you probably are!" Toro spoke with alarm. "You need to get to hospital straight away! I remember seeing something similar in that Ozzy beach rescue show."

"You mean Bondi Beach Rescue?" Reka asked, realising the seriousness of the situation. "I will take him!" She looked outside; parents were starting to arrive to drop off their children for care. "Toro, can you tell them we have an emergency and we can't care for them today?"

Toro went outside to give the parents the bad news, while Reka bundled Kiwa into her car and drove off. At the hospital, when Reka explained to the triage nurse the situation, she immediately sent them through to be dealt with. "He's the second one off that boat!" She said to Reka.

"How is he?" Reka asked.

"We lost him!" was the grim reply. We are trying to get all the others that were on board to come in!"

After observations and an Xray was taken, the decision was made to sedate Kiwa while they tried to remove some of the fluid on his lungs.

Kiwa was then ventilated and taken to ICU, where Reka could only sit and hold Kiwa's hand.

Back at the house, Toro took some time to explain the situation to the parents. Most were understanding and took their children with them, but one mother was adamant, she had no-one else to leave her son with. A little toddler came running towards him, with a beaming smile that Toro couldn't help returning. He noticed casually that Joey had Maori heritage, and wondered where dad was.

"I will see you later, Joey." she said as she turned to leave.

"What time are you returning for him?" Toro insisted on knowing.

"This evening." She threw over her shoulder. "Can you see he's bathed and fed his tea."

Toro could see, that whatever plans he had for the day, had to be abandoned. He felt a little hand grab hold of his finger and pull him towards the play equipment. Toro decided to use the day as practice for caring for Tama. After a little play, Toro took Joey inside the house as the child care centre was locked. He would have to take Joey to the town later for some nappies and clothes. His mother hadn't left anything with him! Toro had a feeling Joey hadn't been fed yet, so he got the toaster out and made some toast fingers with some jam on. Joey ate them with relish! Toro peeled a banana and cut it up for him. That too was demolished along with a plastic cup of milk.

"We're going for a walk." Toro told Joey. Joey made a noise that sounded like he was trying to say walk, and gave Toro another beaming smile. He obviously knew what a walk meant.

Toro took Joey into the room where Tama's pram was kept. He ran over to the pram and tried to say "walk". Toro nodded. He quickly fetched a towel for Joey to sit on and a rug to put over him. A happy Joey was put in the pram and off they set for a walk to town.

They had reached the shops, when Toro met his and Mahina's parents, who were having a look around town before they intended to visit Mahina. There were jokes about how fast Tama had grown overnight, untill Toro filled them in on the situation. They decided to join Toro on his expedition to shop for Joey, which was very helpful, as he had no idea which sizes he needed for nappies or clothes. When everyone returned to Reka and Kiwa's house, they had a good supply of nappies for both Joey and Tama, and also a couple of changes of clothes for Joey, along with a jacket and beanie that Joey loved and didn't take it off untill he had his bath. A teddy and some simple picture books also came home with them.

Toro gave Joey some plastic bowls and utensils to play with while he made a couple of calls. The first one was to Reka, who had to make a quick exit from Kiwa's room to take the call. As she explained that Kiwa was now sedated in ICU, with his obs now stable, she could hear Joey's babble and play in the background.

"Who are you caring for?" Reka asked.

"It's Joey." Toro explained everything that had happened and what he had done for Joey so far.

"You've done really well for him, thank you. By the way, thanks for the advice that Kiwa needed hospital care. One has died and there are three others in the crew who are in ICU with Kiwa. If there is no change, I will come home and have some dinner with you.

"That's good. We've already picked up something for tea. I will give you a call about half an hour before it's served."

Toro then rang Mahina to see how she was going with Tama.

"It's been lots of feeds and sleeping. Have you slept in till now?" she asked incredulously. "When are you coming in?"

"Not at all!" Toro laughed. "Actually I've been getting some practice!"

"What kind of practice?" Mahina was intrigued.

"You will see when I come in! Is it better I come before lunch or afterwards?"

"Come before. We have a rest period from one to three in the afternoon, when there's no visitors."

"We will see you shortly."

When Toro and their parents rocked up, Mahina was surprised to see one of the toddler's from their child care centre, in the pram she had bought for Tama.

"I've got Joey for the day." Toro told her as Joey put his hands up to be lifted out of the pram. He had spotted the baby in the crib and wanted a look. Mahina gasped when she heard of Kiwa's lucky escape from drowning and how Reka was now at Kiwa's side in ICU.

"I'm being discharged tonight." Mahina informed him.

"That's great! But, it's too soon for you to be back working tomorrow!"

"I can do it with your help." Mahina had a determined look in her eyes, that couldn't be ignored. Mahina and Reka had worked so hard to build their business, she wasn't going to risk it by being away when they were needed.

In time they would get a casual carer to help when they were established, but that was for the future.

When Toro's father pulled into the drive of Reka's home, a police car was out the front, waiting for someone to arrive. As Toro alighted from the car, and took Joey into his arms, the police also came over.

"Hello." The officer greeted them. "Is that young Joey Marsh?"

"It is." Toro confirmed as he looked down at Joey, who cuddled into his chest, with a big smile at Toro, which he returned. "Has something happened to Mum?"

"It has. Joey likes you, doesn't he?" Toro grinned at the officer. "I quite like him too! Will mum or dad be coming back?"

"No. He is now an orphan. Are you able to look after him till we can arrange welfare to care for him?"

"Sure. Is there any chance I can become his guardian or adopt him?"

"You want to do that?"

Toro nodded. "If I can."

When Mahina came home that night, Joey was already tucked up in bed after a bedtime story, which became a nightly routine. They discussed Joey's plight. Mahina agreed it was best for Joey to be in a stable family, which he had with them. From that first night, Toro was getting up to Joey for drinks and nappy changes and also for Tama, to change his nappy before bringing him to Mahina for his feed. They both were tired in the morning, but were grateful they now had their new life together. Toro fielded phone calls while Mahina prepared the centre for the day. She had Tama in a sling and was ready to receive the children, when the parents came for the centre to reopen.

# KIWA & TORO'S NEW VENTURE

 Kiwa's condition improved enough for him to be transferred to the medical ward the next day and came home the day after.  Once Reka had returned to help Mahina, Toro was able to start looking for their own place to live, which was more urgent, now that there were four of them sleeping in the room.  Toro also visited the local printer for Some flyers to advertise their business and put an ad in the local paper.  After a visit to the car yard, Koro came away with a vehicle that would serve both the family and the business. A utility with a dual cab and a  covered tray at the back.

A trip to the real estate was a disappointment as there were no rental properties available. They did advise him though, to try the caravan park, where a number of permanent residents lived.  While he was there, Toro asked whether there were any cheap renovator's delights around.  The agent gave him a grin.

There's a couple.  It depends on how game you are!"  The agent gave Toro the details of them and told him to get in touch if he was interested, as he was sure a deal could be done.

At the caravan park, there was a chalet with a deck, which would be ideal, though they would have to furnish it.  Toro promised to bring Mahina for a look later in the day.  A stop at the second hand furniture shop was made on the way home.

Returning to the house, The parents were there. Mahina's mother had Tama in her arms, giving Mahina a break from looking after Tama while she was working.

"We will be returning back home next week." Toro's father broached the subject. "Do you think you will be ready for the ceremony on the weekend?"

"I will be." Toro grinned. "It's up to Mahina, whether she will be ready."

"That's settled then. I will get the iwi to come down.  Reka has said her parents will host the event."

After days of rain, with more forecast, they didn't make a hangi, but large plates of finger food was produced from both Kahi and Lucy's kitchens for a sumptuous lunch.  In front of their parents and Hori's family, Toro and Mahina pledged their troth.  Joey came and hung onto Toro's leg during the ceremony. Afterwards, one of the iwi wanted to know who Joey's father was. When Toro explained Joey was an orphan, he was told Joey was the spitting image of their son who had died.  They had no idea that he had produced a son.

Before the iwi returned to the North Island, a visit was made to the police station at Greymouth where DNA samples were taken, along with some from Joey. Agreement was made not to make any changes to Joey's care until the results were known.  When the results came back as positive, an informal arrangement was made for Joey to live with Toro, with frequent visits from his grandparents and other family members. When Joey was old enough to  join his family in the north, he still kept in touch with and visited his other family in Greymouth.

When Toro's family returned to Greymouth after farewelling their parents, they were now in the chalet. They signed up for six months with an option for an extension.

The Chalet smelt of paint as Toro painted the dining table to give it a new lease on life. He also recovered the dining seats with a cheerful fabric.

Toro knew he needed an extra income to repay the gang. He put an advert in the local paper, to recover furniture. It didn't take long for his phone to ring with enquiries. Most evenings when the children were in bed, Toro would settle down with the latest item he had been given to repair. All of the income went into a separate account.

Kiwa joined Toro on his gardening round, on the Monday morning, to find there was already a regular client base for them to care for. Calls were coming in response to the ads the Toro had put in the local paper, bringing more work to them.

During their lunch break, they had a look at the renovator's delights that the real estate agent had told them about. There was one a few streets away from Kiwa's home that made Kiwa smile. It looked like it should be demolished, but Kiwa could see the potential in this shabby beauty.

"If you don't buy it, I will!" Kiwa challenged Toro.

"How much do you think I should offer for it?" Toro rose to the challenge.

"Put in a cheeky offer of $50K"

"I'm going to need a mortgage. I doubt the bank will give me one for this!"

"No need! I'm good for it. We can set up an account for you to pay me back."

Four weeks later, Toro received word that Settlement had gone through, with details of where to collect the keys.

Toro and Mahina's life was now full. They found they could live on Mahina's income, while Toro's income from the gardening and handyman round went to pay Kiwa for their home.

When the day finally came, several years later, a phone call from Kawa demanding a substantial sum of money – three times the amount Toro had spent; Toro was able to say, "Can I transfer it through to the account as reimbursement of living expenses?" Kawa had no choice but to accept. The Gang no longer had any hold over Toro.

On their first evening at home alone together, Kiwa and Reka sat on the couch by the fire.

"It's nice to have the house to ourselves again." Kiwa said as he took Reka into his arms.

"It is," Reka agreed, as she snuggled into him. "Though it won't be for long." She gave her stomach a gentle pat.

"How long have we got?" Kiwa grinned at the prospect of becoming a father. He had seen how Toro revelled in his role, caring for both Tama and Joey. Kiwa now hoped he would be half as good with his children.

"I had it confirmed today. It is early days yet, so there is plenty of time for us to enjoy our time together."

"Sounds perfect to me."

Kiwa and Reka now had the life they had wanted and the family they had hoped for.

# THE TREASURE CHEST

Amy and Terry took the twins out through the back gate for their now regular walk along the shore. Emily and Jimmy ran ahead of them to see what new shells and rocks had been washed up on the beach. They now had their own section of the back garden for their "treasures".

The twins had their fourth birthday recently, and would be attending Kindy soon. Jimmy found a large piece of driftwood to climb on.

"It's my Castle!" Jimmy declared to Emily. "Dad, can I have my Castle for my garden?"

Terry and Amy smiled at Jimmy's request. He was always wanting to bring pieces of driftwood home.

"I think your Castle may be a little large for our backyard, but we will see."

Jimmy had a determined look on his face that told them that his "Castle" would end up in the back yard, once he found his spot for it.

"What is that Mum?" Emily asked.

She pointed at a wooden object that was tangled amongst the seaweed near the water's edge.

"Stay here."

Amy instructed Emily as she took her shoes off, then waited for the next wave to wash ashore before wading into the water. As she pushed the seaweed aside, Amy recognised the box as an old chest. It looked similar to the one that her great grandmother Emily had brought with her. She quickly stood upright as another wave came in, soaking her legs above the knees.

Amy looked back at the shore, where Terry was grinning at her as he took his shoes off too, before wading into the water to join her.

"What have you found here?" Terry asked, as he felt around the sides for a handle.

"It's Emily's treasure chest. She spotted it."

"Something else for the back garden, if we can get it out of here!" Terry commented as more waves came to soak them. The handles were covered in barnacles, and the chest had to be dislodged from its position in the sand before they eventually carried it to shore.

Emily and Jimmy look on in wide-eyed wonder as their parents brought the chest to them.

"Where has it come from?" Jimmy wanted to know.

Amy looked down towards the river mouth.

"In the early days, there were quite a few ships wrecked as they attempted to come into the river. This will be from one of them. Let's take it home and see if anything is still in it."

Amy and Terry picked up their shoes, to lead the way back home as they carried the chest between them. Emily and Timmy had to be patient till everyone had the sand washed off their feet and their parents had changed into dry clothes, before an old sheet was put down in the family area for the chest to rest on.

Terry and Amy examined the chest. Despite the time it had been underwater, it seemed intact. The lock on the lid also held fast. Terry was wondering what to use to break the lock, when Amy made a suggestion.

"I still have the key to my grandmother's chest, which is similar to this one. I will see if it fits this one too."

Amy quickly ran upstairs to their room for her key. At first there was no movement when she tried the lock. After all, it had been over one hundred and sixty years since it had been used. Amy placed a few drops of her sewing machine oil on the lock. It moved a little, so she tried a few more. The large clunk as the lock finally released its hold was met with a big grin from Terry, a smile of delight from Amy and looks of expectation from the children.

"Do you think there is treasure in there?" Timmy's imagination was running wild.

"No." Amy tried to reduce Timmy's expectation a little, so he wouldn't be too disappointed when he saw the contents. "It will probably be clothing or documents in here."

Amy looked at Emily, whose eyes were still shining at her find. "Are you ready?"

Emily nodded as she came forward to stand by her mother, as Amy and Terry lifted the lid. There was a small silence as they looked at the contents, which by some miracle had remained dry during their time under the sea.

Inside, was filled with exquisite handmade clothes for both a lady and a baby. Amy tried not to think of the fate of their owners, and hoped they had survived the sinking of the boat. In the bottom of the chest, lay a carved box with oak leaves and an acorn carved in its lid. Both Emily and Timmy came forward to see, as Amy lifted the lid. Inside lay a case with two sovereigns and a cloth which held a gold heart shaped necklace with rubies mounted in gold leaves.

"So it had treasure after all." Emily's words were soft and full of wonder as she gazed at the necklace.

"Yes," Terry agreed. "when you grow up, you will have a sovereign each and Emily will have the necklace." Terry looked at Amy. What are you going to do with the clothes?

"I think I will donate them to the museum."

"Can I keep them, Please Mum?" Emily pleaded with her mother, her hand caressing the baby's bonnet.

"If you really want them, then yes you can have them, though they are too nice for dolls dress-ups. We would have to wrap everything in special paper to keep them nice."

Emily nodded her agreement, before Amy packed everything carefully back into the chest. The Oak box was locked away with Amy's own valuables.

The next day when Amy went into the town centre for the acid free paper, she was stopped by Maureen from the travel agency.

"We hear you had a lucky find on the beach yesterday. Was there anything interesting in it?"

Amy smiled that the grape vine was already in action. Someone must have seen them take the chest from the water.

"It had a woman and baby's clothing in it. I had intended to donate them to the museum, but Emily wants to keep them. I will take some photos to show you before they are packed away properly."

"We will look forward to seeing them." Amy realised that everyone in town would be wanting to see the photos, so she took extra care when setting up the display for the photos. Amy enjoyed making the display so much, it gave her an idea for her future career.

When Amy took the photos in to the photo lab in the town centre for processing, she also took a good look round the streets for a venue that would be suitable for the project she had in mind.

She eventually found it. An empty shop with a small front window which she remembered from years ago had a big area inside, which would be ideal. Amy paid a visit to the real estate office. The shop was for sale. The price and the annual rates were reasonable as well. She decided to have a chat with Terry when he came home from the nursery.

Several months later, after much hard work, Amy's new venture was open. In the window, quilts Amy had made were draped around. In the centre was her great grandmother's chest with craft items spilling out of it. A sign proudly announced "The Treasure Chest"

Inside was a display of craft items for sale. Behind the counter, one wall now had shelves filled with bolts of fabric. Another wall had wool and various craft packs to try. In the open space, work benches with chairs all around them had been placed; for the craft classes that Amy had organised. "The Treasure Chest" became a busy place which kept Amy occupied for many happy years to come.

When Amy came home from her first session at the shop, Terry was waiting to take her in his arms for a kiss and a cuddle. He hardly needed to ask how it went. The light in her eyes told him that all had gone well and that Amy had found her new "career" in life. They sat down with the twins who were eager to show them things they had made at Kindy. For both Terry and Amy, their life was now complete.

# ABOUT THE AUTHOR

Born and brought up on New Zealand's West Coast, in Westland, where the Kiwi Kingdom Series is set; Rosemary is a retired Nurse, Mother and Grandmother. Living with her husband in Western Australia, walks in nature, making craft for charity and writing fill her days.

Her mother's love of writing came late – in the 2000's. Writing prose about places Rosemary had visited, was the beginning of her venture into writing. An idea to write a few stories about the place Rosemary came from and the animals that live there, resulted in "The Kiwi Kingdom" being published in 2010. By then, a prequel and a sequel were waiting to be written. They are now incorporated into "Under the Blowholes Spray." Titles four to six have been added to the Series in "The Islands." Now, "Beneath the Long White Cloud" and "The Driftwood Shore" are joining them. Rosemary revels in the joy of creating characters than can be, and do whatever she would like them to be and do.

Printed in Australia
AUHW011211160920
334114AU00007B/14